BLIND SIDED

STEPHANIE CAREY

BLIND SIDED

A NOVEL

STEPHANIE CAREY

Queen of Quirky Publishing
Kansas City, MO

Blindsided
Written by Stephanie Carey
Edited by Cynthia L. Robinson
Book Layout and Cover Design by Cynthia L. Robinson
© 2025 Queen of Quirky Publishing

Queen of Quirky Publishing
Kansas City, MO
helloscarey@gmail.com
www.helloscarey.com

Ordering Information:
Quantity sales. Special discounts are available on quantity purchases by corporations, associations, and others. For details, contact the publisher at the email address above. Orders by U.S. trade bookstores and wholesalers.

Library of Congress Control Number: 2024923629

Paperback ISBN: 979-8-9916662-0-6
Ebook ISBN: 979-8-9916662-1-3

Printed in the United States of America
10 9 8 7 6 5 4 3 2 1

First Edition

For my Aunt Nancy who has always believed in me.
To my niece, Mercy. Dream big!

And, to the heartbroken girlies. It gets better. I promise.
You are enough.

*Fate is fate no matter the timeline.
Some things are just meant to be.*

2001

Sam's head hits something very hard, cold, and solid. She looks around, trying to get her bearings. Three plastic bottles line the ledge of what appears to be a bathtub, next to her head.

Herbal Essences shampoo, conditioner, and body wash. When was the last time she saw that combination of beauty products? She sits up and stares at a purple loofa hanging on a faucet. Clearly this is a bathtub in a bathroom. But it's not her bathroom. She looks at the very purple towel with paisley embellishments hanging on a rack… she's seen that towel before, but it's not hers. She closes her eyes and places the bathroom. It's … her roommate, Dawn's bathroom. Only she doesn't have a roommate. She's 46 and she lives alone with her dog in Kansas City. None of this is possible. Dawn was her roommate in 2001, and this bathroom is in Mill Creek, NC.

She opens her eyes. *How did I get here?* She asks the obvious question to herself. She looks down at her outfit. She's wearing blue plaid pajama pants that she remembers are from Old Navy. They are in much better condition than when she donated them 10 years ago. And does she have a wedgie or is she wearing a thong under these pjs? She hasn't worn a thong in years. These days her favorite underwear would be filed under "granny panty." In addition to the pajama bottoms (and suspected thong) she has on her old favorite gray college t-shirt, which she honestly just donated a few years ago. Her feet are bare. Her toes are painted a light periwinkle blue. She lifts her arms and realizes she no longer has a butterfly tattoo on her right wrist. And she is so, so tiny. She crawls out of the bathtub and looks in the mirror. Holy shit. She looks all of 24. Her freckles pop, but the age spots aren't there yet. Her shoulder-length hair is her natural dirty blonde color... *because I didn't start dying it auburn until 2007.* She stares at her younger face in awe of seeing it again. She notices her eyes are puffy as if she's been crying.

Of course I've been crying. Her boyfriend of two years just dumped her. She's been crying all day. She just took that gummy to stop the nausea she had from the crying headache. But no, she thinks. This younger version of herself doesn't know Frank. This younger Sam would think he was a crusty, dusty old man. This version of herself has been crying because her boyfriend of one year just dumped her. His name being Beau, serving as an ironically tragic side note. *The heartbreak of my 20s that nearly wrecked me.*

She remembers this night and falling asleep in Dawn's bathtub. Earlier she had been looking forward to Beau returning for spring break. He was going to stay at her apartment with her like he had during Christmas break. She went to see a movie, *Someone Like You* with Ashley Judd, with Dawn, and he'd shown up around 10, with his trusty beagle "The General" in tow. She loved The General. He was a bouncy beagle who wandered fairly freely around Beau's college house, and recalled with a special whistle. She thought it was so sexy when Beau put his fingers in his mouth to whistle for the obedient and loyal pup.

Beau and The General didn't stay long that night. Beau showed up and completely blindsided her by telling her he was no longer in love with her, and he would no longer be her boyfriend. Sam shudders remembering the pained conversation she never saw coming. It wasn't really a conversation as much as a declaration …from him. She had given this young man everything of her heart and soul, and he was suddenly, without warning…done.

There had been signs. Of course there had been signs, 46-year-old Sam thinks. The weekend before, she fretted when she couldn't reach him on his house line, even at 2 and 3 in the morning when he should have been back from the fraternity party. But she brushed it off as he was just having a good time. *He probably was having a good time*, thinks older Sam, remembering the cute sorority girls in his circle of friends.

To say she was madly in love with Beau Duvall was an understatement. He was her whole world. He had been her first lover, and she truly thought in her delusional 24-year-old brain she would marry him some day. She even fantasized about playing the part of a southern wife.

She had moved to Mill Creek, NC the previous summer for a job at the daily newspaper, *The Mill Creek Post*, knowing absolutely no one other than the man who hired her named Ed. The second week of her official journalism career, she walked into the newsroom wearing her favorite short stretchy black Express skirt. She paired it with a bright blue polyester button-up shirt that magically never wrinkled, but also never quite stopped smelling like sweat from the hot North Carolina summer no matter how much she washed it. Reporting was often an outside sport.

Sitting across the cubicle aisle in one of the sports reporters' cubicles was a handsome bearded young-looking guy with neat sandy blonde long hair pulled back into a short ponytail. Underneath the beard, he had a defined jawline that could cut. She did not recognize him as one of the sports reporters from her first week at the paper. He was spinning around in the chair absently, as if he had nothing to do, or was waiting on instructions.

"Hi," she said. "Who are you?" Blunt questions were natural to her as a reporter.

"Beau Duvall," he said, standing up and extending his hand. "Newsroom intern for the summer at your service." His accent was sweet and gentlemanly. His smile was captivating. There was a chip in one of his square front teeth that Sam found endearing.

A few days after that, Beau asked Sam out for a drink after work. Despite teasing from the other reporters, she had acquiesced. Over a vodka cranberry she had fallen in love with this southern college boy. He was so different from anything she knew — or any of her previous boyfriends back in Kansas.

She loved everything about him. They both smoked. This is a horrible habit that Sam picked up quickly working in a newsroom where everyone else also smoked. When Sam was with Beau, he would take her cigarette with his in his mouth, to light it for her. This simple move destroyed her every time. He walked with this cocky swagger, despite not being particularly tall. When he kissed her, he held her face ever so gently. No one had ever kissed her like that before.

And of course, she overlooked all of his flaws. Sure, he called his mom "mama," and didn't make a single decision in life without consulting her. His family was from the wealthy part of Mill Creek. He was attending a prestigious southern college that Sam previously hadn't heard of. Apparently it was not quite Ivy League but well established as an academic institution. Then there was the fact that he claimed the Confederate flag wasn't racist but about the independence of the southern states. However, The General was named after a Confederate general. 2024 Sam knows exactly how problematic all of this is, but 2001 Sam was blind to it. She's not proud of this. *Okay, so it's all of a sudden 2001 again and Beau just broke up with me.*

That was one hell of a gummy.

So what, it's March of 2001? Where is Dawn? The memory clicks into place. Dawn discovered a wild hair after that movie. Dawn was the staff photographer at the paper, and she rarely drank to excess. But on this very emotional night for Sam, Dawn left to go drinking with the sports reporters right before Beau and The General showed up and shattered her world. That means…Dawn will be home any moment.

And I should get out of her bathroom.

Why did she get into Dawn's bathtub in the first place? Oh right. She was crying so hard and couldn't find a place where her heart would stop breaking. She remembers thinking, if she got out of her own room, it would somehow hurt less. She must have fallen asleep in that bathtub. Sam turns off the light and enters the hallway where the always leaky air conditioning unit is humming away.

At that moment, the front door flies open and bangs into the wall followed by the sound of a heavy large collection of keys and keyrings falling to the ground and Dawn whisper-yelling "shit." Sam looks at the clock on the cable box in the living room. *How long has it been since she's seen one of those?* It's 3:30 a.m. Dawn is absolutely shit-faced. Her mascara is smeared under her eyes, which are not entirely open.

Sam smiles at seeing the younger version of her old friend again. Dawn remains one of Sam's best friends in life. She and her husband live in Virginia these days. Dawn was even in Sam's wedding to Chad. Sam has a special relationship with Dawn's children who she adores. They had some really good times together, and they still reference this particular night when Sam was heartbroken and sobbing all night, and Dawn came home wasted. Sam knows the iconic moment is about to take place.

Sam suddenly feels like she's in a play where she has cues and lines.

It's showtime.

So, she blurts out, as she did in the first version of 2001, "Beau dumped me. He doesn't love me anymore!" (She almost says Frank but corrects herself quickly.)

Simultaneously, Dawn stumbles forward like a zombie, brushing past Sam, then lurches toward the wall, which she grips for her life before turning to say, "Can't. Talk. Now. Very Drunk. I blame them allllllll." (The last part she says in an oddly growly voice.) She falls into her room with the door closing behind her.

She really should drink some water.

46-year-old Sam has impersonated this moment so many times, teasing Dawn for being so drunk, and herself for being so heartbroken. It truly was the only time Dawn ever let Sam down in the most hilarious of ways. On the rare times they got together in later years, they would drink wine, and Sam would reenact the entry for Dawn, complete with wall clutching and zombie-like stumbling, resulting in hours of giggles. Dawn would return the jabs by making fun of how Sam absolutely lost it when Beau dumped her and sat in their dark apartment watching Almost Famous on repeat.

But dang. Here it is, happening again before her very eyes. *What on earth is she doing here? This has to be a dream.* She pinches herself and it hurts. *A very vivid dream.*

She walks back to her bedroom (because why not?) Turning on the light, she takes a look around. There is a desk against a window with a massive desktop computer setup. *Why did those things have to be so ginormous?* (She thinks of her relatively small iPhone in 2024. It probably has more power than this giant monstrosity.) Her small bed is pushed into the back corner, Laura Ashley floral sheets and comforter strewn about. Tiny clothes are thrown on the floor. She picks up a pair of American Eagle shorts that in 2024 wouldn't fit one thigh. Size 8. She sadly remembers how fat she felt at that size. *Stupid diet culture in the 90s and early 2000's.*

The connected bathroom to this bedroom is equally messy. She sees a familiar green makeup pallet. She forgot about her Clinique makeup obsession. Sephora was barely a thing, so the makeup counter at the mall was next to God for beauty standards.

This is so freaking weird. Also, that's a pretty color. Why did I stop wearing it?

Something on the floor catches her attention. It is a Nokia phone with a sparkly purple case on the back, plugged into the wall next to an old spiral bound address book where she used to keep phone numbers. She can still remember the mall kiosk where she used to shop for cases for this phone. She also remembers the cell phone bills she incurred after this particular breakup. *Brutal.* She picks up the brick of a phone. She hasn't held one of these in decades, she marvels.

What if I take out the sim card so I can't use this to call him over and over again and rack up those horrible bills?

Would that be interfering in the past, causing some sort of butterfly effect in her 2024 life, she wonders. She picks up the phone and tries to remember how to get at the sim card. *This thing is an antique.* She is somehow amused. It was so easy back then to rack up horrible cell phone bills because the minutes were so expensive. She had a very small allotment of monthly minutes, and she would go way over her minutes trying to get answers from Beau, which compounded the problem. Nothing like a little debt to go with heartache.

It's a small gesture to help herself in the big picture. She's justifying and she knows it. She fumbles with the phone. Finally, she secures the sim card and flushes it down the toilet. Probably not the most environmentally friendly thing, but it's all she can think of in this moment of insanity. She pauses. Flushing the sim card is, she knows, a small rebellion, but what she doesn't know is, what are the consequences of this in 2024? Would the butterfly's wings flap this move into something she can't anticipate in her 2024 reality? *Maybe this is all a dream.*

She also tidies up, picking up the snotty toilet paper shreds that doubled for Kleenex in 2001. (Who had the money for actual tissues?) Suddenly the Laura Ashley sheets are looking pretty cozy, and as much as she wants to explore 2001 again, she is notably tired at this moment.

Sam crawls into the old bed, her old sheets soft and worn from college years. This has been the most bizarre experience. She needs to sleep. She will figure things out in the morning… or wherever she wakes up, *whenever.*

2024
Sam's Apartment | Kansas City

Sam wakes up in her 2024 bed to the ping of a text on her iPhone. She's wearing her favorite jammies, and she can tell she's not wearing a thong, thankfully. Her lab/vizsla mix rescue pup is curled up against her. *What the actual fuck was that crazy dream?* On her nightstand, there are piles of used tissues (real ones.) A perk of being in her 40's. She owns boxes of tissues. Or owned. This might be the last box, she thinks. *Tissues and granny panties. The hallmarks of being in your 40's.*

She picks up her phone. It's Sunday morning. Thankfully, it's not Monday and she doesn't have to go to work. The text is just a message from an online boutique where she gave up her phone number for a 10% discount. *I really need to unsubscribe.*

It's still difficult for Sam to go to work for someone else. After her bookstore failed, and she and Chad decided to end their 14-year marriage, she plummeted into an unemployed depression. It took all her might to crawl out of that dark place and put a cheery face on for job searching. Faking the confidence she once had, she endured many Zoom interviews that went nowhere. Finally, a non-profit dog rescue caught her attention. They took dogs from the local shelters and placed them in jails across the state of Missouri where prisoners got to work with and train the pups before they were rescued. They were looking for someone with media experience to run their marketing and public relations – and sometimes cleaning the office kitchen, answering the unmanned front desk phone, and countless other mundane tasks they had no personnel to fulfill.

As if on autopilot, her thoughts turn back to Frank. Yesterday, she thought they were going to go to the art museum, but instead, he called, while walking his dogs – two standard poodles because he's allergic to all other dogs – and told her he couldn't continue their two-year relationship. Specifically, he said, "We need to talk about us." To which she said, "But we don't do that." And he laughed as if it was hilarious.

To say she was shocked is an understatement of grand proportion. He didn't really have any solid reasons and spewed a lot of cliches like, "It's not you. It's me." Honestly, she had been as blindsided as she was when Beau Duvall broke up with her, after she had just watched an entire Ashley Judd movie about breakups.

Old cow, she thinks. A reference to Ashley Judd's character's obsession with a cow theory in relationships. The theory is that men are like bulls, and they require a new cow after mating. The old cow is… discarded. The movie is actually based on a book Sam read called "Animal Husbandry" by Laura Zigman. Like most adaptations, the movie did not live up to the book, but Ashely Judd is adorable throughout the film. She breathes in deeply, inhaling how much she loves Frank. She had been, is still, intoxicated with him. The way he could change the whole trajectory of a day with one simple text, "hi." *He's not going to text me "hi" anymore.* Her eyes start to fill up with tears. *Oh no.* She cried enough yesterday to end up over the toilet because her crying headache turned into nausea. She cried enough yesterday to send her orbiting back to her 24-year-old self.

She also can't help but think of her poor 24-year-old self back in 2001. The next morning after the drunk Dawn incident, she had called the only person she knew would be awake at 7 a.m. on a Saturday morning. Amy.

Amy was the mother of the newsroom. Her job was a hodgepodge of some pagination, obit work, and she served as a liaison between the advertising department and the newsroom. She also happened to sit in the entry to the newsroom so she had to talk to a lot of community members who came in to complain about the news, or share some wild story they thought should be covered.

Sam's favorite version of Amy was when someone referred to the paper as the *Evening Post* (It had been the *Evening Post* up until 1995 when it turned into a morning newspaper and rebranded to The *Mill Creek Post.*) Most of the time, Amy wouldn't bother correcting folks. But, on days where that one person just pushed Amy over the edge of southern politeness, she'd very aggressively correct them, "Sir, it's the *Mill Creek Post*," Amy would snap. Sam always knew Amy would need a smoke break shortly after those moments.

Amy was 10 years older than Sam, but you'd never know it by looking at her. The first time they went to lunch together and Amy drove, Sam had been surprised to see a child's car seat in the backseat. She had asked if Amy babysat. Amy laughed and said it was for her son, which Sam obviously didn't know she had. Amy soon took Sam under her wing like a big sister.

And since Amy had a toddler in 2001, Sam had known she would be up early that morning. She got in her old 1992 Audi, a hand-me-down from her father, and a much nicer car than she deserved to drive on her salary. She'd sat on Amy's kitchen floor sobbing while Amy made muffins for them. It is such a core memory for Sam. She remembers feeling devastated and hopeless, but also so very loved by Amy, and the confused toddler who didn't understand why the lady from mommy's work was crying on their kitchen floor. He kept bringing her his Matchbox cars.

Now that baby is 25.

She's reminded of Frank and his almost adult children. He is such a devoted dad, which is one of the things Sam loves about him. Sam doesn't have children of her own. She was always chasing her career as a journalist, and she and Chad never wanted them. Frank is the first dad she's ever dated. He's also the first man she's dated who works in manual labor. She finds his work for the railroad to be incredibly sexy. She remembers lying in bed at night hearing the sounds of the train horns and thinking of Frank out there somewhere driving a great big train. It sure was a helluva lot more interesting than some guy's boring sales job.

Sam needs to get her life together, but everything in her apartment suddenly reminds her of Frank. The outfit hanging on her door is what she wore the last time they saw each other. *Just a few days ago.* She spies the stuffed elephant he got her because she loves elephants. If she were to walk into her living room, she'd see the loveseat where they spent hours snuggling. They were watching Ted Lasso, and they were somewhere in the second season. *I'll never know what happens to Ted.* She coughs up a sob. *Now I'm crying over Ted Lasso.*

Should she text him? *Oh no. This is just as bad as my behavior in 2001 with the expensive cell phone minutes. I cannot repeat that behavior.*

It did me zero favors then, and it will do no good now. Wow, look at that maturity. No one has to take her sim card away, she swallows satisfied, and then grabs her phone and starts composing a text.

Oh, this is mad. I cannot be this sad over a goddamned 47-year-old man. She thinks of his hands, rough from years of work with the railroad and his gentle smile, always a little sad around the edges. The truth of the matter is he's not ready to be in a relationship because he's not over his wife. They were married for over 20 years, and she sprung a divorce on him out of the blue.

Sam has always known this. She just hasn't wanted to admit it to herself. She thought she could somehow win his love, but it was always just out of reach. Yet somehow Frank's devoted interest in her life made her believe they were a real thing. Sam thinks she drove the relationship forward on the dream of him falling in love with her. *Forward like a train. The train has reached the station and will not be continuing service.*

Suddenly it dawns on her… 24-year-old Sam knew what to do when she was down bad. 24-year-old Sam phoned in a friend.

That is exactly what 46-year-old Sam should do right now before she starts sending off texts she doesn't need to send. She picks up the phone to call Donna. Donna and Sean are friends of hers from her short-lived bookstore days. They own a small business in Kansas City – a jewelry store, that barely made it out of COVID days alive, but is still going thanks to the tenacity of Sean and Donna. They were never huge fans of Chad, so Sam happily kept them in her divorce. They've really seen her through a lot of grief and trauma. But they also really liked Frank.

"Oh my God," Donna says when Sam breaks the news about Frank.

"That asshole," Donna mutters.

Sam has not yet reached "anger" so she starts to defend Frank, "I mean yes, but he has a lot going on and you know, his ex…" She trails off.

"Stop defending him, Sam!" Donna exclaims. "You need to get your butt over here and have some dangerous margaritas and tacos." (Donna makes the best pan-fried tacos anyone has ever had.)

"SEAN," Donna yells off the phone. "Sam's coming over for dinner and drinks. Start squeezing those limes because Frank just dumped her and she's going to need one of your margaritas stat." She hears Sean yell, "damn!" in the background. Then back into the phone Donna says, "Please Uber here."

Sam laughs. She knows she has absolutely no choice but to get her "butt over" to Donna and Sean's.

****

Sam loves Sean and Donna's cozy house. Ever since she had to leave the house she owned with Chad – and he'd kept, Sean and Donna's house has been a refuge from her tiny apartment. Even Millie loves playing in their fenced yard.

Over tacos and "dangerous" margaritas, Sam pours her heart out to her dear friends. They are a few years older than her, and Sean had a few marriages before meeting Donna, so they offer an empathetic ear. Much like the time she cried on Amy's kitchen floor, Sam blubbers like a baby when describing the breakup and wonders out loud how she is going to survive.

She leaves out that she recently time traveled to her 2001 self in another state.

"You just need some fresh D!" Sean says mischievously after his second margarita. Donna laughs and slaps him with a napkin. "Stop it, Sean."

Sam blows her nose with her own napkin, which they placed in front of her, along with her margarita when she arrived.

"Well, you aren't wrong," she laughs. It feels good to break the monotony of weeping to just giggle a little.

Sean and Donna are her safe place, her refuge, just like Amy was all those years ago.

On the way home in her Uber, the familiar streets, buildings, and lights all blur. She cannot believe this is her reality right now. How is she so heartbroken about a man she wasn't even married to? No one told her this would hurt more than divorce. Sam pulls out her phone. Tequila wrecks her willpower, and she composes a text to Frank.

"You shouldn't have dated me when you were still in love with her. You broke my heart, and it's not fair," she sends through blurry tearful eyes. Then she immediately regrets it.

Fuck it.

"And furthermore, Sean and Donna think you are an ass for breaking up with me while you were walking your damn dogs."

Frank does not reply to her unhinged texts.

****

A few days later, Sam is sitting at a bar near her apartment, drinking a glass of pinot noir, fighting the urge to text Frank something funny that happened at work that day. So far she has not experienced any residual consequences from the flushing of the sim card when she was back in 2001. Although, Dawn did text her randomly the day after she "time traveled." Maybe the whole thing was just a weird dream. She's always been a vivid dreamer.

There is no way she actually time traveled to 2001 after taking a gummy. Perhaps this is something she should bring up in therapy. It can't be normal. Frank said he admired her for going to therapy, but he wasn't ready to go himself yet. Sam tried to encourage him to find a therapist, but how could he with his schedule? *If he wanted to, he would. Maybe I could send him just one last text. For closure.*

She slams the phone on the bar, wipes a small tear with her bar napkin and looks up to catch the bartender watching her. She's a tall, slender, heavily tattooed younger woman who knows Sam's drink order (it changes seasonally.)

"Going through it?" the bartender asks. Sam sighs. "That obvious?" "It's okay," the bartender says as she dries the glass she has just washed. "I think Mercury is in retrograde so we are all going through it."

Sam smiles. She loves how sweet the "gen Z" generation is.

Two glasses of pinot noir later, she walks home to take her dog on a walk, feeling no pain for a glorious moment. She has to be strong tonight and not text Frank after this wine. Maybe she should take a gummy and just go to sleep.

She remembers the last time she took a gummy. *That was a wild trip. Surely it can't happen again. Maybe it had something to do with that Mercury in Retrograde? Honestly, it was probably just a dream.*

2001
The Hole in One Pub | Mill Creek, N.C.

S am is sitting on the toilet in a very dirty bathroom with writing on the stall wall. It smells of cigarette smoke and a very strong musky air freshener. She stands up and pulls up her thong underwear – *again why?* – and then down her very short jean skirt, smoothing it out. She steps out of the stall and looks in the mirror. The same young version of her face greets her as the last time she took a gummy. (Oh, she wants to tell this version of herself to put more sunscreen on her nose so she doesn't get sun bumps in her 40's) She has paired a skin tight yellow tube top with this short skirt and is wearing platform flip flops. There is a little glitter in her eye shadow. *Where am I?*

She knows it's Mill Creek, NC 2001, but she can't place this bathroom.

She washes her hands while singing Happy Birthday to herself (Covid habit) to make sure she is thorough. Using a paper towel (this place is gross), she pushes open the swinging door and steps into The

Hole in One, a pub the sports reporters used to love drinking at after deadline. They talked a big game about getting the ladies but really all they did was play the Golden Tee golf-simulation video game for hours on end.

Sam always thought they liked playing Golden Tee because they were all sports-star wannabes who wrote about sports because they couldn't play sports. Golden Tee was the outlet that scratched that itch for them.

"It's about time," Rob, the sports editor says when she emerges from the bathroom. "What. You taking a gigantic shit?"

 Sam rolls her eyes. They were so pedantic.

"No, she says, only slightly annoyed, "I was powdering my nose."

"Let's take a shot!" Loren says. Loren is the newest member of the sports department. He just moved to Mill Creek from Texas. He did an internship at one of the company's sister papers down there, so he thinks he's big time. He is in the process of getting the "Mill Creek humble,"- come in confident then realize you know absolutely nothing about journalism, or life, and that you are going to have to work your butt off to get out of Mill Creek and onto something bigger.

Everyone at *The Post* had aspirations of going bigger. Back then Sam had her eyes on the *Atlanta Journal Constitution* because it would keep her and Beau in the south, and wouldn't be too far from his mama.

"Absolutely not," she says to Loren about the shot. Rob gets a wicked look in his eyes and orders up four Wild Turkey shots. "Hey, Jack," he shouts across the bar to Sam's boss, the lifestyle editor, who is playing a game of pinball in the corner. Jack is the kindest soul, but also the most cynical man Sam has met to date. He doesn't believe in love and had just kind of grunted when Sam had told him Beau broke up with her. It's honestly fun to see Jack again. He went on to be a Managing Editor at a metro-wide paper in Pennsylvania, surviving many cuts to newsrooms and consolidating papers over the years.

Ugh, she remembers this night. She drank so much Wild Turkey that Jack had to hold her up. Then he had to pull over so she could throw up in a parking lot. She was such a puker back then.

She stops to take in the bar.

It is poorly lit with two pool tables, a dart board, pinball machine, and the ultimate destination: The Golden Tee game. The bartender is wearing jean shorts that barely cover her ass, and a white cropped tank top that shows off her belly button ring.

She produces the four shots of vile liquid.

Oh god. Sam remembers the wine she had before the gummy and doesn't know if it's that, or whatever young Sam drank before she materialized in the bathroom, but she is already tipsy.

"Everyone take her easy — but if she's easy, take her twice." Loren says lifting one of the shot glasses. Rob and Jack take their shots and lift them to touch Loren's. Everyone looks at Sam who is already starting to get nauseous thinking of the acid she is about to pour down her throat.

Despite her hesitations, she lifts the shot and touches it to the boys' shot glasses before grimacing and downing it. She gags and coughs but keeps the shot down.

Loren looks at her with a wicked smile and says, "Pussy," jabbing her with his elbow. Sam thinks this must have been the kind of energy that Dawn faced the other night hanging out with these bozos.

Why had she thought they were so cool back then? Look at them. *They are so young.* They really are just a bunch of boys searching for their path in life. Jack would continue to be a grumpy editor, but he'd be damn good at it, making a name for himself among the press associations. Rob would go on to other sports departments, but Sam thinks he settled into a public relations job himself. Possibly for a sports organization. She remembers he got married and had twins. That's what Facebook told her, anyhow.

She lost touch with Loren. She never liked him much. She thinks it's because he sat in the cubicle Beau once occupied. *Guilt by cubicle association.*

Two things about Sam: she wears her heart on her sleeve and she's an inherent over-sharer. The whole newsroom knew about her heartbreak back then. It might have had something to do with the open weeping she did one afternoon at her desk until Amy took her outside to "get some air." On this first weekend post-breakup with Beau, the guys had begged to take her out. With no other plans, Sam had agreed, and here she is.

Here she is in 2001, standing in a pub that may no longer exist for all she knows. *I'll Google this when I return to 2024.*

"SCORE!" Loren yells from the Golden Tee game. "This means another shot!" he shouts loud enough for the bartender to hear while he faces the game, his hand on the little rolly ball that lets the player launch the pretend golf ball toward the pretend hole.

Sam steps over to the bartender and whispers, "Hey. Can you put some water or ginger ale or something other than wild turkey in my shot?" she asks. Hopefully this will help Sam the next morning and prevent the vomit-a-thon out of Jack's car. The bartender winks at her and says, "I got you!"

Sam sips on the Miller Lite her younger self must have ordered before she got here. *It's not bad,* she thinks. *Kind of refreshing.* She rarely drinks beer in her 46-year-old life. The shots are produced. Sam delivers them to the boys so she can hold onto the imposter shot.

It's so weird to be out without any connection to the rest of the world. No one in this group of hooligans has a cell phone on them. They are all just here. In this moment. For Sam, this moment again. *What are the odds of this being another vivid dream?*

After downing the "shot," she walks over to Jack, the most reasonable one of all of them. Jack is a little older and certainly wiser than the rest of the Golden Tee gang.

"How are you doing?" he asks softly. He knows about Beau, and despite the unsympathetic grunt he gave when she told him (to be fair, he was working on his pages at the moment) he truly cares.

Sam shakes her head, "Not great." She thinks about Frank. She smiles knowing he'd absolutely love this bar. He loves old dive bars. She thinks he wouldn't be able to order his IPAs here, but she bets they have PBR, his second favorite beer. She feels her stomach sink.

Jack gives her an awkward side hug. "I don't talk about it much," he says, "But before I moved here, there was someone…" he trails off. "Damn it," he says and takes a long pull of his Rolling Rock. "Well, let's just say, I know something about losing someone you love," he states matter of factly, trying to erase the pain from his voice with a false bravado. *That is so Jack. It's so good to see him again.* They started at the Post around the same time, but he wasn't her boss when they first started. As newbies to the newsroom, they hung out a lot. Then, her boss got an elusive job at a bigger paper and he was out of there. So Jack stepped up for the promotion. It was a little weird at first because he knew so much about her as a friend, and then he became her friend turned boss.

"It was so out of the blue," she blurts out. "I never saw it coming, and he told me over the phone while he was walking his dogs!" *Oh shit.*

Jack looks confused.

"I thought he just had that one racist confederate dog," he says "And how does one walk a dog and talk on the phone? Was he using a cellular phone? That's so expensive!"

"Um, sorry, yeah. He was walking The General and um…he has a really good cell phone plan that his mom got him." She hopes Jack will buy this.

Loren comes over again with shots. Sam looks over at the bartender who shrugs as if to say, "Sorry I tried."

Sam puts her Miller Light on the cocktail table and takes the shot in her right hand.

"Here's to being single, seeing double, and sleeping triple," Loren says.

"You wish," says Rob after downing his shot and wiping his mouth with his arm.

Sam feels the room get a little spinny, so she holds onto the side of the tall cocktail table next to her.

"Yummy!" she says in fake excitement. "And absolutely no more." She's really trying to take care of young Sam's body and well-being while she's…invading? She's really not sure what's happening with this gummy and finding herself in her 2001 body reliving her 2001 life, but honestly, she's starting to really like the nostalgia of it all.

TLC's "No Scrubs" plays and, Sam, who is feeling that shot kick in, starts singing along and wiggling in her short skirt. The GoldenTee gang egg her on to keep dancing. She knows she is safe with these guys, but she thinks about how vulnerable she is as a young woman out with all these dudes, not to mention all the alcohol.

Oh my god. I am such an old lady thinking these things!

Jack walks over to check on her. Then he leans over and whispers, "If he doesn't love you, he doesn't deserve you. He's spoken, and he meant what he said. The door is closed now. I know it's hard, but take it from me. Don't keep trying to open that door. You'll only get hurt more."

Oof. It's a hard thing to hear. And even though Sam knows Jack is talking about Beau in 2001, her heart breaks for Frank in 2024.

2024
Sam's Apartment | Kansas City

Sam wakes up in her 2024 bed with a headache and her phone pinging with a Facebook notification. She's not sure if it's the wine from this timeline, or the shots from 2001, but she knows she deserves this. The night ended with Jack (who probably shouldn't have driven, but that's what they did in 2001) taking her home, hopefully not as drunk as she was that first time around. She had not puked in a parking lot, so she feels pretty good about how she left young Sam.

She checks Facebook and sees that the ping is a friend request from Loren of all people. *Strange. I literally haven't spoken to him since the day I left the paper.*

And now she needs to work. How can she write press releases about prisoners training dogs when all she can think about is her broken heart and her adventures in 2001. She remembers that she actually did some of her best reporting right after Beau broke her heart.

She poured her emotions into her writing, and dug deep with her sources to get them to tell her their real thoughts and feelings about the topics she was writing about. One of those topics was a program for fathers who got behind in child support but still want to have a relationship with their children. It was a complicated issue facing the less fortunate who get in a bind with child payments.

Sam thinks of how hard Jack was on her about deadlines around that time. He absolutely would not let her broken heart get in the way of her producing stories for the features section every day.

She starts thinking about how she loved telling Frank about her adventures with her job, visiting the prisons in Missouri, and seeing the inmates work with the dogs. He listened with so much interest. He was so different from her ex-husband Chad, in so many ways. Frank's interest in what she would have previously considered mundane details of her life never ceased to amaze her.

 She and Chad had this dream of a bookstore that could feature local and indie writers, and maybe serve beer and wine.

It was weeks away from opening when Covid hit. They lost everything, and Sam had to freelance to pay the bills. Chad had quit his job to work on the bookstore with her, so he had to find another job. Then, they were just stuck in their house together for months. She remembers feeling like she was suffocating in his presence. Sometimes she would wake up early just to go downstairs and have alone time while Chad slept. She remembers the way her stomach would drop when she heard sounds of him awake and moving around above her on the second floor. The Covid months of solitude together may have been the final straw that ultimately broke their marriage.

To be honest, the marriage hadn't been great for several years. There is a particular pain that is the fading of a relationship over many years. You kind of grieve as you go. So, when they were done, Sam was sad for the life they built together being over, but she wasn't romantically devastated. The love had been fading for some time, and she was finally facing it. She knew Chad would remarry because he absolutely can't be alone, but she didn't know about herself.

Then she met Frank…Frank the guy who opened car doors for her, and never said a negative word about her parents. Even Sam's father loved Frank.

Sam looks at the container of gummies. There are still a few left. Should she take another? Would it send her back to 2001? In 2001 she thinks about Frank a lot less, and helps her younger self with the Beau break up a lot more.

She feels herself welling up with tears and thinks, *yeah, I have to get out of here.*

2001

The Post Newsroom | Mill Creek, NC

The noise of many landline phones ringing at once is jarring to Sam who is used to the polite way that people's individual phones ring in people's pockets or bags back in 2024. There are quiet conversations being had in cubicles and corners, and a tension fills the air. Welcome (back) to the newsroom, Sam. *At least I'm not in a bathroom this time.* Sam surveys the large Apple Macintosh computer on her desk. She has no memory of how to operate this beast.

She scans her desk which is covered in reporter's notebooks, file folders of paper, and the AP Style Book. *What am I working on?* Can she help younger Sam finish this story? And if she fumbles the ball, will it mess with her present timeline in 2024? She still hasn't figured out the consequences of her gummy-induced time travel. *Was that friend request from Loren on Facebook supposed to happen?*

It's been so long since she's written anything but press releases and social media posts. An entire feature story about something seems daunting. Hopefully this is one of those easy stories where the sources come to you and it's all feel good and fluffy.

Jack looks over their connected cubicle glaring at her. His dark brown hair is messed up which means he's been rubbing his head, which he did when he was stressed. *Uh-oh, he's mad*, Sam thinks.

"I don't give a fuck if your story fell through. You need to produce a story for Sunday's paper, and I need it by tomorrow morning. So figure it out," he barks.

"Also, I don't care if the love of your life dumps you, or your hair catches on fire, or any of your other drama. Get it done."

Sam grimaces at the hair reference and reflexively reaches up to touch her hair. Yup, absolutely shorter than when she was in the pub with the sports guys. She must have "landed" after the incident when she'd caught her hair on fire while trying to light a cigarette with a match. To her credit, she tried to continue working, but the dramatic reaction in the newsroom from the sports reporters' covering their noses and gagging from the smell of burnt hair sent her straight to her hair stylist to get it cut off, but also take her layers into consideration. Like she couldn't just run to a nearby Great Clips and get it fixed quickly. She had to go see her stylist. 46-year-old Sam groans at her younger self's lack of professionalism.

Unfortunately, she was on deadline at that moment, and poor Jack was sitting back at the newsroom waiting for her to fix her stinky burned hair so she could finish writing her story. *Laptops would have been so convenient in situations like that.*

Wait! She knows exactly what story this is. She was supposed to do a profile on a local pastor and his contributions to the greater community. It was to be a wholesome Sunday Lifestyle piece. It would have needed some good portrait photos by Dawn to round it out. But it would have been easy to knock out. Unfortunately, the pastor got called away to a sick relative and had to cancel the interviews and photo session. It left Sam scrambling to find a new story.

She remembers combing through piles of press releases looking for something. Anything. Every day, all day, the newsroom fax machine would churn out press releases. They would automatically drop into a bin, where Amy would eventually sort them and distribute them to the reporters per their "beat." Sam organized all of her press releases in a file folder.

On that day she rummaged and finally she found a press release from a big box grocery store, of all places, saying their parking lots were now open for RV travelers to camp overnight. Sam thought that was a novel idea, and it could be a cute story. Oh, want some late-night ice cream? Just get your slippers on and head on into the superstore straight from your camping spot! DoorDash wasn't a thing yet. She thinks about how easy it would be to find someone in 2024. All you'd have to do is open up TikTok and look for the RV and van life community.

In 2001 Sam had to go about things the organic way: find folks in the wild. But her 2001 self didn't know if anyone would be camping in the Mill Creek store parking lot tonight. It was a huge gamble. She legitimately could have gotten fired if she didn't produce a Sunday feature story.

But what 2024 Sam knows is there will indeed be a couple camping tonight. They won't get there until 9 p.m. or so when Sam would be on the brink of a nervous breakdown, driving to the neighboring town's store to check for campers there. But on her very last time circling the Mill Creek location, as she will be convinced her career is in the toilet, they will be there. Not only will they not be serial killers, they will have a beautiful story to tell.

She can relax for a minute and soak in the newsroom. She sees Amy working away across the room and after making eye contact, gives her a little wave. Amy hesitates and waves back with a perplexed look on her face. Sam realizes they don't normally wave at each other randomly. Usually, Sam would get up and stand by Amy's desk to gab for longer than Jack's watchful eye approved.

She turns toward the offices where the managing editor and the city editor sit. All seems quiet on that front. Deadline is hours away. *Maybe Amy wants to go to lunch at El Rancho.* She knows she certainly wants to go eat lunch at Rancho, as they called it. So, she gets up and walks to Amy's desk. As she does, she takes in her outfit: khaki capris from The Gap, Steve Madden chunky black slide sandals that give off a suction noise with every step she takes, and a short sleeve button up from Express. *Ahhh, so early 2000's.* Once again, she feels the sensation of a wedgie, but she knows it's not. It's just her damn thong underwear. *Should I buy my young self some granny panties? If younger me can get over the stigma, I feel like I'd really appreciate the comfort.*

Sam briefly hopes her bank account is up to supporting this lunch she's about to purchase. Then she gets to Amy. "Hey, Amy. Wanna get out of here and go to lunch?" They never have to say El Rancho. It's always the only option.

Amy looks up from where she was paginating the TV guide section, one of her most hated mundane tasks, Sam remembers.

"I'm knee deep in Jeopardy to Golden Girls," she says. "But okay!" She jumps up and grabs her purse. "Who's driving?"

Even though El Rancho was only a few blocks from the newsroom, they always drove. Sam has no idea the condition of her car, or even where she parked it that day (not that it'd be hard to find), but she freezes at the question.

Amy looks at her funny and then jangles her keys, "Don't worry. I'll drive. I just got gas this morning!"

At El Rancho they pick the smoking section. Sam reaches into her purse and pulls out 2001 Sam's package of Winston Lights. *Ew.* She smoked them because Beau Duvall smoked them. She gave them up, switching back to Marlboro Lights a few months after they broke up, but apparently not yet. She enviously eyes Amy's Marlboro Lights. "Do you want one of mine?" Amy asks without looking up. She can apparently feel Sam's longing for the better smokes.

"Yes," Sam nods. "All these do is remind me of Beau," she adds. They are entirely too strong for someone who hasn't smoked in a while. Amy nods sympathetically. The previous summer, Amy, Sam, and Beau had enjoyed smoke breaks together. Amy knew Sam had started smoking his same brand of smokes. She even commented about it once.

"So how are you doing with the breakup?" Amy asks as she lights up. Sam also lights up, coughing a little at the burn of the cigarette on her lungs. She quit smoking several times over the years, but she's weak when presented with the option of cigarettes.

Sam thinks about Frank, and how she took a gummy just to avoid the pain of him. She wonders how he is, and what he's been up to. She really misses their constant texts and inside jokes. Like the time she found out he had been going to a tanning bed before a trip to Mexico with his kids.

"A tanning bed?" Sam was both amused and appalled. "That's the most 1990s thing I've ever heard."

Frank laughed and said, "I never wanted you to find out."

"Then why did you tell me?" she asks perplexed that her manly, blue collar boyfriend was engaging in such a vain activity.

"Because you asked me what I did today and I forgot to censor my answer around my embarrassing guilty pleasure," he said.

"And like an actual tanning bed that you crawl into and put the lid down? Not like a spray tan?" Sam asked, needing to confirm the information.

"Yeah, an actual tanning bed. I like the way it makes me feel all warm and cozy," Frank said sheepishly before folding his arms across his chest and pretending to shiver for dramatic effect.

"Well, I guess you do look…tan," Sam responded in a fit of laughter. "Do you have one of those bunny-shaped stickers on your hip?" Frank put his head in his hands as if he couldn't with her.

Back in 2001, sitting in a smoky booth with a bowl of chips and ramekin of salsa placed in front of them, Sam answers Amy's question. "I am getting by, but it's really hard to focus on anything other than how sad I am."

The truth.

Sam realizes that in this weird second time around moment, she is now older than Amy. It sort of shakes her in a way. She decides to ask about Amy's marriage. Amy didn't talk about her relationship very often, but Sam knows that in 2024, Amy is divorced and living in

Chapel Hill. Maybe she can offer up something helpful, or just listen and hear Amy in whatever she wants to share.

When the waiter comes around, Sam orders a cheese enchilada and bean burrito combo. She doesn't even have to look at the menu after all these years. In the years to come, Sam would often crave El Rancho, thinking no other Mexican place was as good as the family-owned Mill Creek establishment.

"So how are things with you and," Sam hesitates because she almost can't remember his name but reaches deep into her memory and finds it, "Tom?"

Amy rolls her eyes. "Well. You know he's unemployed at the time being. And you would THINK he could help out around the house while I'm working away at obituaries all day, but nope. When I get home, the house is as tore up as I'll get out." she sighs and takes a drink of her water.

Sam nods empathetically. She knows how the division of labor can often be skewed in a marriage. But young Sam doesn't know that yet so she can't say that. Instead she says something worse. "It's giving real househusbands of Mill Creek," she says without thinking anything in that sentence through.

"Giving?" Amy asks, raising her eyebrows. "What's giving? And what is a real house husband?"

"Sorry," Sam stammers. "It's just a thing they were saying at my college," Sam hopes this doesn't sound like the lie it is.

"Why would your college friends be talking about husbands of Mill Creek?? Oh never mind. What's your big Sunday story this week," Amy asks, changing the subject.

Sam gives her the gist of the story, thankful to be relieved from explaining her futuristic colloquial phrase.

Amy scrunches up her face. "Sam, your story is due tomorrow. That seems a little risky if you don't even have sources yet." As designated mother of the newsroom, Amy always knew everyone's deadlines. "What can I say?" Sam says brightly. "I love living on the edge!"

Amy's face remains scrunched. "That doesn't sound like you. Are you okay? I know this breakup has you in a bad way, but you can't be taking this kind of risk with your job!"

Sam smiles loving how Amy has her back. *Amy was such a good friend.* And she wonders how Amy is doing in 2024. She hasn't seen her in a few years.... not since her last trip back to Mill Creek in 2018 for Ed's retirement party. Ed was the editor of the paper who hired Sam. Amy reached out in 2018 and invited Sam to come to the retirement dinner, which was held at, none other than El Rancho! Sam and Chad had argued about whether or not they had the money for her to fly to Raleigh, rent a car, drive to Mill Creek, and stay in a hotel for two nights.

2018 Sam won, but Chad would bring it up over the years as an example of how life always revolved around her needs. Chad never understood how fundamental Sam's first reporting job was to her existence. It truly defined her.

Back in the newsroom after lunch, smelling like an ashtray and someone's fajitas that passed by, Sam approaches a sober young Dawn who is working on another giant Macintosh. She is looking at photos in what Sam can't help but note is a very early version of Photoshop from a photo shoot at the library. Digital cameras were a brand new thing. Right before Dawn started at the paper, they still had an active dark room for processing film.

Dawn is wearing jeans and a fitted black top. As a photographer she got away with a little more casual wardrobe at work. It was fair because she often had to climb around or lie on a dirty gymnasium floor to get high school sports shots.

"What's up?" Dawn asks, not looking up from the screen as Sam hovers over Dawn's work.

"Up for an epic adventure tonight?" Sam asks. Still not looking up, Dawn asks, "What kind of epic adventure, Sam?" Her tone is skeptical because she's probably used to Sam's great adventures to nowhere.

"A superstore adventure!" Sam responds.

"We don't need anything at the apartment," Dawn says practically. Of the two, Dawn was always the most frugal and level headed.

"I know that," says Sam. "I have a story." Feeling the need to appease, she adds, "Trust me. It's good."

It was a close call, but luck was on my side.

When they got to the parking lot for one last drive by, there was indeed a camper parked toward the back of the lot. While Dawn waited in the car, her own Nokia at the ready to call 911, Sam had bravely walked up to the RV door and knocked while saying "knock knock" aloud in a cheerful tone. 2001 Sam was so fearless.

An older man answered her knock. Sam had explained she was with the local newspaper and she was writing a story on the store's new camping friendly parking lots and could she interview the man and have her photographer take some photos? The man smiled and welcomed her inside. Sam remembers turning to Dawn with a thumbs up and a little waving motion that she should join her.

The couple inside the RV did have a story to tell. They were traveling the country with their son's ashes. He passed away in a motorcycle accident. They were scattering his ashes in all the places he never got to visit, and Sam remembers another detail. The couple called Kansas City "home." She had bonded with them over that. "It's a really good story," Sam says.

2024
Sam's Apartment | Kansas City

Sam is back in her cozy 500 square foot midtown Kansas City apartment. Her TV is on a streaming service, but the screen display asks if she's still watching. She ducked out of 2001 before she and Dawn could have their parking lot adventure. So far, in her Marty McFly-like adventures, she's figured out that she has about 4-5 hours in 2001 before she somehow automatically returns to 2024. She hypothesized that the gummy wears out. The times she's been awake to experience the return, she's observed that her vision gets blurry and all the background noise fades. Then she's back in 2024.

Her apartment is small and lacks any character, but it's an affordable apartment. And it has a dog yard for her dog, Millie to run around in. She and Chad had lived in a house a mile or so west of her current place. The good thing is, she can walk to about a dozen bars and restaurants, and she doesn't even have to park on the street. Sam is terrible at parking. In fact, she's not even that great of a driver.

She appreciated that Frank let her be the passenger princess during their two years together. She figured if he could drive a train, he was absolutely safe to drive her in a Toyota Camry.

Nothing in her apartment is out of place or unusual, so once again she thinks she must not have messed with the past too terribly much. She checks her email, and there is a message from a recruiter who wants to know if she's interested in a reporting job in Chicago. *Reporting job? Why would I be interested in that? Is this what I get for the butterfly effect? Job inquiries?*

Millie has to go out, so she slips on her Vans and takes the leash off its hook on the wall. Outside in the yard, Sam sits on one of the two janky lawn chairs placed for residents to sit while their dogs are in the yard. She opens her phone and thinks about what she would love to say to Frank at this moment.

"Hey Frank. I miss you so much. I've been time traveling back to my old self in 2001 and let me tell you. It's been a wild ride!"

Yeah, then he'd really call her crazy, she thinks. Frank always referred to his ex-wife as "crazy," and he teased Sam about how she was also crazy in her own way.

I guess my "crazy" stopped being cute. Sam stares off into the yard until another thought enters her mind.

But I am cute. I'm really cute. You know what? I'm so cute, I should download the dating app again right now so everyone will know how cute I actually am!

Just days ago, Sam had been proclaiming she'd be single for the rest of her life.

Before she met Frank, she was on the apps, and she had dated a few guys. Nothing went anywhere.

But this one Sunday, her brother Jason's band had been playing at a honky tonk in the West Bottoms of Kansas City. It was a cute venue that hadn't been updated since the middle of the last century and still retained that vintage western charm. Her bestie, Timothy, was supposed to accompany her to this particular show on a Sunday afternoon. But Timothy bailed. Timothy often bailed because Timothy would party hard, meet a guy and go underground, so to speak, for days. Then he'd come back up from his sex den, or whatever it was, and text, "Bitch. When are we getting together?!"

So that day, Sam had been flying solo. She had been sipping on vodka sodas and vibing to the music when a tall, dark, and handsome man with several piercings in his nose and a row of them up each ear, appeared next to her. He looked kind of familiar, and Sam realized she had matched with him on a dating app a few weeks prior. She was instantly attracted to him. But since his profile was kind of boring, lacking any witty intro, she hadn't had anything to say to him. He expired from her matches 23 hours later.

But, suddenly he was live and standing next to her watching her brother sing on stage.

Sam dug deep into her big girl brain and found the most creative line she could think, "Come here often?" She literally embodied the facepalm emoji in this moment.

"Yeah, I actually do," Frank had replied. Then he set his beer down and extended his hand, introducing himself as Frank. She returned the handshake. His hands were worn from what she would later learn was years of railroad work.

Sam would also learn that Frank liked to visit this establishment for live music any Sunday afternoon he wasn't out at work. His job took him to various locations, a day's train ride distance away, where he'd spend the night and return on another train after 12 hours of rest.

Sam then told Frank that the band currently playing starred her brother as singer. And if he was single, he should put her number in his phone. She might have repeated herself a few times because of the vodka sodas.

At the end of her brother's set, she had intended to catch a ride home with Jason, but Frank offered to take her home.

Sam had asked, "Are you a serial killer?'

"If I was, would I admit it?" Frank had responded with a twinkle in his green eyes – such a rare color.

So Sam had agreed to have a total stranger take her home, but only because as the band was packing up, she marched Frank up to her brother and introduced them.

She loudly announced to the entire band, "This is the murderer if I go missing."

Jason was used to her antics and laughed at her. "Had a few drinks during the show, Sam," he had jabbed at her. Then he shook Frank's hand and said, "Take good care of her, man."

"Take good care of her" *For a while he had.*

On their way to Frank's car, Sam's brand new white cowboy boots hit some loose gravel, and she lost her footing. She tried to stop her fall, which only made it worse because she toppled down and landed on her right knee. To her horror, the gravel had cut into her and blood was trickling down her leg into her new boots.

"Woah," Frank said as he tried to help her up off the ground. Sam stared at her now bloody leg.

"Oh my goodness. How embarrassing," Sam said out loud.

Frank was unphased and just quietly helped her into his car. "Hold tight," he said and then disappeared to the back of the vehicle. Sam was mortified. Then she heard sounds of the trunk opening. For a very, very brief moment she wondered if he was going to put her in the trunk. (She watches too much Dateline.) Then Frank reappeared at the car door with an entire medical kit.

Sam watched in shock as he proceeded to wipe off the blood, and clean it with an antiseptic spray. Then he procured a rainbow of band aids with varying designs. He fanned them out like a deck of tiny cards.

"Do you want unicorns, butterflies, squids, or Spiderman," he asked without a hint of irony in his voice.

"Um," Sam said, absolutely flabbergasted. "Where did you get these?"

"I have kids," Frank said. "They are too old for these band aids, but I can't give them up." Then he smiled, as if he was in his own memories. "They were so cute when they were little. And trust me, we used the hell out of this kit."

"I love butterflies," Sam responded, and he went to work placing the band aid on her knee. Sam could only stare at this man who so gently applied the butterfly band aid. "Thank you," she finally remembered to say.

"No problem. Jason?" he inquired about her brother's name to make sure he had it correct. Sam nodded.

"Well, Jason said to take care of you. I take my responsibilities very seriously." He closed her door and went around to the driver's side.

Sam was literally falling for this man within the first 20 minutes of knowing him.

Back in the dog yard, Sam is already in the app store looking for her preferred app and trying to remember which email address she signed up with originally. She connects it to Facebook and *voila!* She's back in business with a two-year-old, but fairly strong profile. She scrolls through her pictures and omits a few, replacing them with newer ones so no one can accuse her of catfishing.

"Let's see who's out there," she says as she starts to scroll.

An hour later, Sam is frustrated and totally over it. "Troll Date," she mutters. She and Millie return inside where she sees the bag of gummies on her counter. They look so tempting to get her out of the pits of despair she finds herself in. *Where did Timothy buy these anyway?* And now she wonders if she takes one, will she go back to 2001, and what will her 2001 self be getting into this time?

2001
Hotel Bar | Mill Creek

What she would be getting into was absolute trouble. Sam is seated at the bar next to Rita, the free-spirited copy editor who rolled up to the newsroom in a VW van one day asking for a job. Turns out, she had tons of newspaper experience, and there was an open position on the copy desk.

Half-empty martini glasses are placed in front of both Rita and Sam. The bar is empty except for them, and a dude who is paying his tab. Sam instantly knows what night this is. She groans, causing Rita to take a long sip of her drink and say, "You've really got to snap out of this. There is absolutely no man worth being this sad over, cupcake!"

But right now Sam isn't thinking about Beau or Frank. She's remembering…the Cowboy.

At that moment, a not-so-tall, not-so-handsome guy in a cowboy hat, western shirt complete with pearl button snaps, jeans, and cowboy boots walks into the bar at the Holiday Inn.

Oh Shit. Her younger self could really use some discretion. He is a lot hotter in my memories.

It's not that weird that Sam and Rita are drinking at the Holiday Inn on a Saturday night. There aren't that many places in town to drink, and The Holiday Inn bartender specifically knows how to make a martini to Rita's liking.

Rita had made it clear all over town that no one else knew how to make a martini. Rita was not shy about anything. During a staff meeting about new health insurance, she had shot her hand up and asked how much a popular medicine for erectile dysfunction cost on the new plan.

The sweet HR lady didn't know the answer or even how to respond to this aggressive question. This drug was still relatively new to the market back then.

"Because my birth control is at the highest tier of this price listing, and I just want to know if men have to pay as much to have sex as I do."

The sports reporters snickered. Sam remembers the HR lady wringing her hands as she tried to stay calm and reply that she didn't have a full list of medications and what price point they were at, but if Rita needed to know, she could find out. (Spoiler: the ED medicine was indeed cheaper than the birth control. Points for Rita.).

It's Sam's turn to take a big sip of the salty booze in front of her.

The cowboy sits down next to her asking if the seat is taken. Sam shakes her head no then turns to Rita wide-eyed. "What do I do?"

she mouths.

Rita smiles and nods encouragingly. She doesn't know that what Sam is really asking is "do I interfere with this Canon event in my life?" smiles and nods encouragingly. "You fucking talk to him, babe." she whispers. She leans closer and lowers her voice more. "Then you fuck the shit out of him and get over that stupid little beau of yours." Sean's comment back in 2024 about needing to get some "d" pops into Sam's mind.

Rita downs the rest of her martini and proclaims, "I'm beat! I'm going to head home and see if my man wants to get it on!" Along with a van, Rita had a domestic partner in tow with her when she arrived in Mill Creek.

She winks at Sam and sashays out of the bar toward the parking lot.

She just glides everywhere she goes. Sam briefly wonders about Rita in 2024. She can't even remember her last name, which is sad since she's probably someone who has no idea the impact she made on Sam's life.

Sam turns to "the cowboy" who is now seated next to her and has ordered a PBR beer.

Great…because I really need to be thinking about Frank right now.

Sam knows she has a one-night stand with this average looking cowboy. She also knows exactly why he's sitting in a Holiday Inn bar on a Saturday night looking for trouble. He's rolling through town with his uncle to fetch some cattle. His uncle, she remembers, is sleeping in the hotel room they are sharing while Mr. Cowboy is out looking for play.

But what she doesn't want to have to do is sloppily make out and have what she remembers is really bad sex with this idiot. She does thankfully remember a condom being involved.

Beau had been her "first" partner, and the sex had been, well, she didn't have anything to compare it to at the time. Looking back, she thinks it was as good as it could have been. The sex with Frank had started off awkward but evolved into a blissful connection she looked forward to. Is it because she is getting older, and knows her body better? Probably. But she also thinks there is more to it than that.

Back in her current present she wonders if her 24-year-old self needs to have this one-night stand. In her first timeline, it is literally a pivotal event in her moving forward out of love with Beau. The next time she would get with a guy, it would be her next long- term relationship.

Woah woah woah. She cannot think about that one right now. She needs to figure out what to do for young Sam right now, in this moment, *again*. Actually, what she needs to do for young Sam is order another stiff drink and make the cowboy pay for it, she thinks.

She sticks to the script and asks him the questions she already knows the answers to. He has deep brown eyes and his face tells the story of acne-prone teen years. His crooked teeth are not at all endearing like Beau's.

Then 46-year-old Sam asks, "So what do you want to do with your life?"

Good grief. Mom mode much?

"I don't know," he responds. Then he gets a sly grin and adds. "I'd like to do you."

Sam cannot help but roll her eyes.

Wherever he is in 2024, he is at least age appropriate, so this isn't creepy, Sam tells herself.

"No, but you really should have a plan," she continues on the career counseling path.

"Ok, so what's your plan?" he asks her.

"Well, my ultimate goal is to own a bookstore," Sam says and can't believe she just shared that. Then again, she is an over-sharer.

The cowboy nods. He's starting to look a little bored.

"Have you considered the railroad," Sam asks him?

What am I doing?

"Like working on the railroad?" he asks skeptically.

"Yeah, like an engineer driving the train, or being the conductor where you are responsible for everything outside the train and watching out for the engineer," Sam says. Then she adds, "You know, it pays really well!"

"You like money?" he asks.

"I mean who doesn't," Sam says, "But no, it would be a really good job for you."

"And how do you know so much about the railroad, Miss Reporter Lady?" he questions, a hint of mockery in his voice as he acknowledges her job.

Why am I trying to give this guy career advice and why am I thinking about Frank's job?

"I wrote a story about the railroad," Sam lies. Then she tacks on, "And I think working for the railroad is kinda sexy."

Hello, vodka talking.

He breaks into a big smile and takes a drink of his whiskey. "Now you're talking my language," he says as he puts his hand on the skin below her very short skirt.

Clearly he's not interested in career advice tonight.

An hour later, she is indeed making out with the cowboy with bad teeth.

I am 46 years old. I am making out with a 20-something year-old cowboy at a hotel bar in Mill Creek, N.C. This has to be a new low for me.

The bartender clears his throat loudly, causing Sam to break away from The Cowboy. This man is clearly not impressed by this scene. "Last call," he says. "Closing time…." the cowboy sings into her ear, his tongue flicking her seductively.

And that is when Sam, who is suddenly very turned on – the ear always does it for her – remembers that she doesn't have a car now. Rita left in her van, which leaves her officially without a ride.

"Oh. My. God. I call Jack for a ride," Sam remembers, horrified. She did. Dawn was out of town visiting her boyfriend, now husband, and Jack was the only other person in Mill Creek Sam could think to call for a ride in her booze-fueled attempt to fuck the first thing that paid

attention to her.

Nope. Officially found a new low.

"Um sir," she says in her polite tone she reserves for people in authority, to the bartender who probably didn't mean he was willing to serve them another drink. Just that he wanted them out of his bar. "Could I please borrow your phone?"

In 2024 this would never happen, but here in 2001, Sam knows she shouldn't use young Sam's precious minutes up and she needs to call Jack. She takes the Nokia out of her purse and scrolls her contacts until she sees Jack's name and a number. The bartender hands her a cordless phone with an adjustable antenna. "Here," he grunts.

Sam cross-checks Jack's number as she dials. Meanwhile, the cowboy is getting frisky as his hand climbs up her leg and under her short jean skirt. She bats the hand away playfully.

Jack answers on the second ring. He sounds annoyed with a hint of amusement on the edge of his tone.

"Jack. It's Sam."

"Since when do you live at the Holiday Inn?" Jack asks, acknowledging what must have come up on his caller ID.

"I um don't. I was here at the bar with Rita, and she left..."

"She left? Why would she leave you alone?"

"I'm...not exactly alone." Long pause.

"So you need a ride, I take it," he says dryly.

"We do," Sam responds.

"*We?* Good lord, Sam. Well I hope he's, I don't know, not a murderer," then he pauses. "I guess if he is, I'll have the inside scoop on a nice, juicy news story. I'll be there in ten." He hangs up. Sam is left listening to the dial tone, a sound she hasn't heard in a while.

Sam pushes the "off" button on the phone and hands it back to the bartender. She turns to Cowboy and puts on a big smile. "All good!" He responds by leaning in to kiss her some more. The bartender clears his throat again. "We should wait outside," Sam whispers to Cowboy.

At least I know I'm wearing sexy underwear for this encounter. No granny panties for young Sam.

Despite the awkward experience of having her boss pick her and her hook-up at the bar, Sam feels like she's getting the hang of her time travel adventures. Maybe it's the vodka, but Sam feels totally in control of her ability to return back to 2024. Little does she know, the hold she thinks she has on these abilities is about to completely unravel.

Sam is thankfully spared the bad sex back at the apartment scene, but she is not spared the ride of shame from the Holiday Inn back to said apartment. No one says a word. Well, the cowboy says, "thank you, sir" to Jack and Jack says, "have fun! See you at work on Monday" with a smirk as he drops them off. Sam pines for the anonymity of Uber.

2024
Kansas City

Sam exits her Uber and looks for the entrance to the agreed on establishment. She's exactly on time for a first date with an average looking middle-aged man who works in IT by day. She is probably not as excited as one should be for a first date. But she is looking forward to hopefully not thinking of Frank for a few hours. Or, 2001 for that matter.

Tech guy has beaten her to the bar and is seated. He does not stand when she approaches, which is disappointing because she's so used to Frank's old fashioned manners. But he does greet her warmly and he looks like his pictures, so that's a plus.

Sam knows she probably should have run this guy by one of those groups on social media to find out if he has known red flags, or a wife or girlfriend. It's unfortunate, but so many guys pose as single when they have whole-ass families at home.

But since a quick online snoop revealed they have a few mutual friends, and the friends they share are pretty solid people, Sam decided to hold off on posting in one of the vetting groups.

She also knows assuming he is "one of the good ones" based on the friends they have in common is delusional in 2024. But maybe she is just a little delulu right now. Here she is on a date just two weeks post- absolute heartbreak. Look at her! She's so strong and moving on, she tells herself. It's almost working.

Frank who?

Tech guy is easy enough to chat with. They quickly play the "how do you know" for their mutuals. (He must have snooped on her as well.) After that, they settle into the first date ritual of exchanging random facts about themselves. Sam thinks Frank already knows all of these things about her. She shouldn't have to share them again!

And in that moment, she has crossed into the "thinking about Frank" threshold. She excuses herself to the bathroom where she leans in to talk to herself out loud in the mirror.

"Get it together. Do not think about Frank. He's just a loser who was never good enough for you to begin with." Then she adds, "Tech guy probably makes more money!" She is not shallow in the way that she chases money but that is the best jab against Frank she can muster in the moment. Frank is certainly more attractive to her than Tech Guy, so she can't use that against him figuratively in her mirror self- talk.

She returns to Tech Guy with a smile. He's seriously so nice, but he's just not Frank, she thinks. At this point she knows she is a failure at rebound dating, and it is time to call it a night. One would think making out with a cowboy two nights ago would have gotten Frank out of her system, but apparently that distraction was only meant for young Sam to get over Beau.

"Hey," she says to Tech Guy. "I'm sooo sorry to rush off, but I need to feed my dog." She knows this is the most ridiculous excuse, but it's all she can come up with. She's already thinking of the bag of gummies back home and an excuse to get out of her current reality. He quickly grabs the server and pays the bill. *Very generous considering my abrupt need to flee this date.* Out loud, she thanks him. Then she pulls out her phone to order an Uber. (She cringes, remembering Jack pulling up in front of the Holiday Inn in his beat-up Saturn the other night.)

She puts in her location and waits for the little app to find a stranger in a car to drive her home. She continues to chat with Tech Guy who is also ordering his Uber. This is an awkward part of the date because should she go in for a hug? A kiss? She has no clue, so she stares down at her phone. *Oh good! A driver has been found.*

A few minutes later the largest, tallest pickup truck Sam has ever seen pulls up. "I guess this is me," she says to Tech Guy with what she hopes isn't absolute panic in her eyes. Somehow she has to get her ass up into that thing. He laughs at the size of the Dodge Ram in front of them. "That is an uber Uber!" he says.

Sam tries to play it cool but trips a little and has to hoist herself up in the cab an extra time because she doesn't land the first attempt. She hopes her butt looks cute in the black flared jeans she's wearing. She waves at Tech Guy and is on her way home.

The relief is too big not to notice.

Now with a few drinks in her, and a date behind her all she wants to do is text Frank who knows her and could laugh with her about how awkward it was when she couldn't get up in the cab of the uber truck. Sam thinks of all the time Frank drove her home after dates. How she loved kissing him passionately in front of her gate, neighbors be damned. The way he would turn around one more time as he was walking back to his car and wink. It would cause her to melt.

Why am I consumed with this man? She remembers the deliciousness of being home after a date with Frank. She was never drained or worn out. She was always just so happy and hopeful for the next time she could see him.

The truth of the matter is they never fought. He had his teenage kids – a boy and girl –and his busy job at the railroad. Despite his schedule, they always found time to be together. Sometimes they would go a few days in- between visits. Others, a few weeks. But it was always just so easy whenever they would come together. The constant texting kept them connected in between dates. She loved his little check-ins and his commentary from the road.

One time, he had been in a van taking what's known as a "deadhead" from one location to another. "I swear this driver is trying to kill me. This might be my last text. I'm sorry. Tell Millie she is a very good girl, and you're ok too," he had texted her. That was the closest he ever got to expressing his feelings toward her. A winky emoji here, a reference to her as "his girl" there, but never an "I love you."

In fact, on their one-year anniversary when Sam had been so sure he was going to confess his love, he didn't. Sam even tried to prompt him, "Can we talk about our feelings? I'd like to share a few thoughts." Frank had quite literally clutched his invisible pearls against his chest and looked stricken. "Please no," he said. Sam's cheeks had burned in humiliation. *Even Beau said he loved me.* She remembers the tanning bed conversation, and wonders if hitting the tanning beds in his free time was the only secret Frank tried to keep from her.

I really thought he was so honest with me, but I have evidence, actual evidence that he wasn't.

They were regulars at a vintage-style Kansas City establishment with tin roof ceilings, marble floors, and a beautiful original bar with ornate detailing that made the liquor bottles seem even to sparkle more. All the bartenders knew them by name and their respective drink orders. Sam ordered the martini; a drink she credits Rita to this day for introducing her. Frank ordered his IPA. Then they just tuned out the world for a few hours and talked. Sometimes touching hands or legs or both. Every once in a while, engaging with the bartenders for some banter but always slipping back into their private world of conversation. She had never had such easy conversations with any other romantic partner. Sam had never complained he couldn't stay late, and had to get back to his kids, because she was thankful for the time he did share with her. She told him that often.

Then they would walk, swinging hands, back to her apartment and have the farewell kiss at the gate.

Sam is thinking in circles now. Her therapist would say she is ruminating.

She pulls out her phone and shoots off a text to Tech Guy. "Hey! Thank you again. I had so much fun. Sorry I had to rush off. Would love to see you again. Oh, and I had to tuck and roll out of that truck!"

He immediately responds with a "haha." And her rumination is broken with the quick hit of dopamine she gets from that text. Ok, maybe she can go on a second date, she thinks. Let's give dating in general a chance.

She opens Troll Date and begins swiping left. For each photograph she sees, she imagines what the guy in the photo would be like on a first date.

Her first date with Frank had been nothing short of magical. She knew they had chemistry from when they met at Jason's show, but she didn't know if they had anything in common because…well, she couldn't remember exactly what they talked about on the way home. Most likely, she probably spent the time thanking him for the first aid and apologizing for being such a klutz.

But when they sat down for that first date, it was like she had known him her whole life and they were just catching up after not seeing one another for a long time. They even both had the same hyper fixation about climbing Mount Everest. Sam's fixation focused on wanting to interview people who climbed it, while Frank's interest leaned more toward actually risking his life to climb it. Sam joked that if he didn't die, she could do a story about him. The date went so well that Frank had called in for work or "laid-off" his next trip, as the railroaders called it. They ended up making out in his car in the parking lot and fogging up the windows like teenagers.

She is ruminating again and knows she needs to stop. Good thing she knows a sure-fire way to escape her thoughts. At this point she feels like a real life professional time traveler. Too bad the gummies will run out soon. *Better enjoy them while they last.*

2001
Mill Creek
Sam & Dawn's Apartment

Sam and Dawn are on Dawn's couch watching TV. Well, no, they are watching *Almost Famous* or probably Sam is watching it and Dawn just joined her. Sam isn't sure. It's the scene in the bus where they sing Tiny Dancer and Sam always cries.

Dawn hits the stop button on the remote control for the DVD player. When the movie is silenced, Sam can hear the leaking air conditioning unit rattling away in the hallway. At one point, the leaking got so bad the carpet in the hallway became saturated with water, and they referred to it as "the swamp."

"Ok, ok. Enough sulking. Also, I'm pretty sure you could own this DVD now with all your late fees to Blockbuster for not returning it." Dawn states.

Sam rolls her eyes. She did make a mess out of her Blockbuster account. *RIP Blockbuster.*

"You know, your brother is coming to visit and you haven't planned anything to do with him," Dawn says. Oh yeah, Sam thinks. *Jason did come to visit me right after Beau broke my heart…well a few weeks after.*

Sam and Jason are not "close." Their five-year age difference paired with a gender difference and the fact that they have very little in common aside from mutual parents doesn't help either. In 2001, Jason had been in college in California and their parents had told him the only place he could go for spring break was either their house or to visit Sam. He had chosen to visit Sam only because visiting one's sister was slightly less horrific than going home for spring break.

"We could take him to the beach," Dawn suggests. "Or maybe into Raleigh? I think they have some good museums. Does he like museums?"

Sam shrugs thinking of her little brother as a small boy running around a museum on a family trip to Chicago. "He liked museums as a kid, I guess."

"What about bowling?" Dawn continues.

"Absolutely not bowling," Sam says. "He used to crush me in bowling as a child, and my ego cannot handle the massacre at this moment in time."

Dawn gives her the look. The look that Sam knows Dawn employs on a daily basis with her kids in 2024. That look could make the cockiest sports writer go creeping back to his desk if he dared to critique her photos.

Sam thinks she should take Jason to see some local music but then remembers…the 2001 music scene in Mill Creek is not ideal. *What did they even do the week he visited?*

"Just think," Dawn says, "This is your chance to spend an entire week with your brother. When will you get this kind of an opportunity again?"

Wow. Dawn has no idea how right she is at this moment...

They never would have another week together. After college Jason would marry his high school sweetheart and buy a house in a suburb of Kansas City where they both grew up. In 2024, Jason is still married with three kids. He owns a business where he does some kind of consulting. Despite living a few miles away, they only see one another at holidays and maybe once a summer at their parents' lake house.

Sam loves being an aunt, but between the bookstore and then, her divorce with Chad, and busy schedules, she hasn't always been the best aunt.

Jason met Beau once when Sam brought him home for Thanksgiving. They only stayed two nights because of Sam's schedule at the paper, but Beau and Jason had quickly hit it off better than Jason and Chad ever did over the years.

She really wishes she knows her brother better now and then. All of a sudden Sam realizes what she needs to do in 2001. "All of it," she says out loud.

"All of what?" Dawn asks, confused.

"Let's do everything. Let's drive to Nags Head and walk on the beach and get a beer from that one new brewery we saw last time we were there. Can Jason even drink yet? I don't care. And let's explore the entire Raleigh area. Then, we can go bowling and take him to hang out with the sports guys one night!" Sam is so excited she begins to ramble.

She needs to make young Sam an itinerary for when her brother comes to town so that she won't fail at this plan.

Sam runs to her room and surveys the mess. She must have been worse off than she remembers because the room is trashed. She probably hadn't had any energy to pick up after herself. Sam grabs a notebook and returns to the couch to map out a schedule starting the next day when she is supposed to pick-up her brother at the airport. She pauses for a moment and realizes it's possible to go all the way to the gate to pick him up. *9/11 hasn't happened yet.*

An hour later, she has an entire schedule mapped out for her brother's visit. She smiles. So far none of the changes she's made in 2001 have had any "butterfly" effect on her present life. At one point she worried she'd start to erase herself like Marty McFly started to do in *Back to the Future.* But every time she is back in 2024, things are still the exact same, lonely heartbreak and all.

But are they? She thinks of the random friend request from Loren, and the email from the recruiter.

She wonders if she should tell her brother that when he plays in the show at the Honky Tonk in 2022, he should NOT invite her. If she doesn't meet Frank, none of this heartbreak happens. She could even write Jason a letter with DO NOT OPEN UNTIL 2022 written on it. *That wouldn't be weird, right?* She decides to ignore her impulsive thoughts.

Sam makes sure she puts the itinerary in a prominent place on young Sam's nightstand so she won't miss it. She also shows the entire thing to Dawn who she knows will keep young Sam in check if she doesn't deliver on this plan. Dawn scribbles her initials next to the activities she plans to join them on.

"It sounds like a fire plan," Sam says.

"Fire?" Dawn questions with a very skeptical look on her face. "What's on fire? Your hair?" Dawn thought the burned hair incident was hilarious, and she agreed with the sports guys about the putrid smell.

"Oh, it's something I just heard at one of Beau's fraternity parties. I thought I'd try it out," Sam lies once again and hopes it works.

"Yeah, I don't think anyone is going to be saying "fire," Dawn says. "Nice try though."

They will in 2024.... You know, I really should call Dawn and the fam in 2024.

"Anyway, it's good to see you excited about something," Dawn says. "I feel like you are coming back alive."

Sam goes to sleep in young Sam's floral bedding that night knowing she will wake up in her 2024 reality, but also satisfied that she left young Sam a week of new memories with her little brother.

2024
Kansas City

Sam stares at her laptop, trying to write a press release, but she cannot focus. She cracks a mini Diet Coke. *Why are these so delicious and the perfect size.*

She opens a blank document.

Dear Frank, she types. Then sighs and continues.

It's been a month since you ended us without warning. I just wish you could have shared your doubts about our relationship earlier. Maybe we could have talked about it. I know you miss me. I mean, how can you not?

She stops. How can he not miss her? She is truly the best thing he had going in his life besides his kids. How can he stand this time and space between them? Why isn't he writing letters to her apologizing for ending a relationship that was only happy times and wonderful? She thinks about what her therapist would ask her. "What made it so wonderful?"

Well, they never fought, for one. They never ran out of things to talk about. They liked the same 90s music and even traveled to Columbia, Missouri to catch a live Ani DiFranco show, his birthday gift to her the second year they were together. His love of Ani had been one of his green flags for Sam. *How can you love Ani DiFranco and not be a feminist?*

He took an interest in Sam's favorite books and read them while he was on the road so they could discuss on their dates. It was like a cute little book club of two. They were the perfect food sharers at restaurants, always agreeing on what to order and splitting plates so they could try more items. He made her laugh, but she really made him laugh. He actually found her funny and not annoying, the way that Chad had during their marriage. It was so nice to make someone laugh.

They just "got" one another. She thought their chemistry was off the charts. They were always touching, kissing, and staring into one another's eyes. She thinks back to the breakup conversation over the phone when Frank had said "I just don't feel chemistry with us right now." The dagger he twisted in her heart with those words. She tries her best to not relive those words over and over in her brain, but sometimes she wakes up with them in her head.

I just don't feel chemistry with us right now.

She opens a new document and names it, "Two for Smoking." Two for Smoking is the idea for a novel she never wrote. The one time she told Chad about it, he said it probably needed more flushing out. It's inspired by her friendship with Amy, told over a series of lunches at El Rancho in the smoking section. It highlights their age difference and the powers of female friendship over the years. After seeing Amy again in 2001, Sam realizes there really is something to this book idea of hers.

But then her ADHD kicks in. She has another thought and decides to look up Beau on the old Facebooks. She types "Beau Duvall" into the search, and he pops up. He looks exactly the same as she remembers, with that intense jawline and some gray in his beard. His hair is shorter, but still a little shaggy. She thinks of Beau spinning around in that chair at *The Post* on his first day in the office. She hovers over the "add friend" button.

Should I do it?

After Beau broke up with her, they had several long phone conversations that cost Sam an arm and a leg, but they never saw one another again. Sam remembers seeing him driving in Mill Creek once in the car his mom bought him. By then she was already dating Jeffrey, her boyfriend of six years before she met Chad. Jeffrey was a failed stockbroker who lost his job shortly after 9/11 due to layoffs at his company. She met him at a friend's Kansas City wedding back in July of 2001. He moved to Mill Creek in October of 2001 and they were together for six years of absolute terror. Jeffrey was literally the toxic relationship Sam should never have had. He was the opposite of Beau– and even later on Chad, and Frank.

Of all her past lovers, Jeffrey was the most toxic. Their relationship did not end in her heartbreak, but it did end in a lot of broken dishes and furniture that he smashed when he left. It also led to a lot of debt because he wasn't so good at keeping a job, and Sam held them together for a few years on her meager journalism salary.

Sam clicks "add friend" under Beau's photo and holds her breath. A few minutes later she gets the notification that her friend request has been accepted. She opens up Messenger and starts to compose a message to the first man who truly broke her heart.

"Hey, thanks for accepting my friend request. How are you?" she types.

She sees the dots that indicate he is writing back. She holds her breath thinking of young Sam and how much she wanted answers after the breakup. Answers that Beau could not give. *Answers that Frank cannot give.*

Beau Duvall: Hey! Good to see you. I'm doing well!

Sam: Are you still writing?

Beau Duvall: Yes! I'm in public relations for a private school. I've been here over a decade now.

Sam: Oh cool! I too am in public relations. I guess that's where all good reporters go when newspapers die on them. Ha ha.

Beau Duvall: Ha ha indeed. At least you worked for one professionally. I never got past "intern."

Sam: Please do not remind me that I dated the intern 😅

Beau Duvall: You did. And he was still in college!

Sam: Stop. Remember my first fraternity party with you? I was like what am I doing back in college. I just graduated!

Beau Duvall: No, but I remember you getting drunk at one of our parties and giving all the sorority girls career advice. I had to drag you away.

Sam: Ugh. That sounds like me. So do you have any dogs these days? I have a lab mix. She's 8 and her name is Millie.

Beau Duvall: I do! I have two huskies and they are absolute nut cases.

Sam: Oh, I hear huskies have a lot to say!

Beau Duvall: Seriously. They never shut up.

Sam pauses. *What would young Sam want to know that would help her with closure from Beau?*

Sam: So I'm working on a book loosely based on the newsroom gang.

Beau Duvall: No way! That's rad!

Sam: So anyway, I was wondering if you could share a little bit about your perspective from when we broke up.

She closes her eyes as she types "when we broke up"
This is embarrassing.

"You know, a million years ago," she adds and holds her breath while watching the chat box.

No reply dots.

Then reply dots.

No reply dots

Then reply dots

She waits for 10 minutes and then gets the response she's been waiting 23 years to get.

Beau Duvall: Ah yes. I think about that sometimes. I really surprised you with that one, and then I had absolutely no answers for you. I believe I loved you. But you were just so focused on your career and I wasn't sure I could stand by for all of that. I also just didn't think I was ready to get married, and I thought I should let you go so you could find someone else. Truthfully, Sam, you were so great, but I had a lot of growing to do. I just didn't know how to express myself back then. I thought it was best just to end it before it got too hard for me.

Truth bomb, Sam thinks.

Sam: Was there anything I could have done that would have dissuaded you from ending our relationship?

She sucks in a breath as she waits for him to reply. 2001 was a long time ago, but in Sam's current situation, it seems to be not THAT long ago.

The dots dance.

Beau Duvall: Probably not. I was pretty set on it. I remember being relieved when it was over. I hope that's not mean to say.

Sam: Not at all. I mean, kind of, but it's water under the bridge now! I just needed some information for perspective in my novel. I want to be able to write from a place of knowing more than my character.

Beau Duvall: Yeah, a book about *The Post* sounds fun. Let me know when you have a manuscript.

Wow, Sam thinks. Young Sam is going to cry so many tears for Beau Duvall over the months that follow their breakup. And all the while Beau Duvall made his mind up just like that.

Did Frank dismiss me so easily?

Sam decides to be responsible and not take a gummy to avoid her thoughts. Instead, she opens TikTok on her phone. What did the FYP have to say to her in this moment?

Very quickly Sam discovers that the algorithm of TikTok is surprisingly creepy and accurate. She is on break-up TikTok.

There on her screen, a close up of a woman's face. "What do you do when the avoidant dismisses you?" the woman asks.

Sam swipes up for a new video to appear.

She sees a close up of another woman's face. "Let's pull cards tonight for someone who is separated from their person. The separated person is deeply regretful and longing for the one they've discarded. I see..."

Sam does and doesn't want to know what this tarot reader sees. It's not based in reality. It's all based on her desires and biases. She knows this, but her yearning to hear someone say Frank misses her and regrets ending things with her burns strong. They are words she would nearly die to hear. *If they were true.*

What would the tarot readers think of her bouncing back and forth between 2001 and 2024 by taking gummies that Timothy gave her? Actually, Timothy said he'd never take one of those gummies ever again. There's this lady on TikTok they call "Auntie Matrix" who tells people's supernatural stories and glitches in the matrix.

Well this is certainly a glitch in some matrix.

There has to be a reason for this time travel. Like a life clue or a lesson for Sam in the present day. Because so far, nothing Sam has done as past Sam has changed her present-day life. There were those coincidences – the text from Dawn, the friend request from Loren, the email from the recruiter. But she has no idea if she thwarted a mega cell phone bill in 2001. She still remembers it as such. She also doesn't know if she ended up doing all those fun things she and Dawn planned with her brother. Her memories remain dim and blurry, but she hopes she did those things with her brother.

****

A few days later, Sam has successfully avoided taking any more time warp inducing gummies, although she's been tempted. Tech guy has stopped returning her texts, so she continues to swipe away on the app. She's also made a big step to change Frank's name in her phone to "Dog :poop emoji: Pick Up" It's a silly edit, but she's so used to seeing his name with the train emoji she put next to it, and associating it with the joy of a text from him.

And she no longer gets texts from Frank. The thought saddens her. Timothy told her to delete the history, but that's just not something she's ready to do. Two years of daily texting, checking in, and making each other laugh. Many, many good mornings and good nights. Aside from the few selfies she has of them, this is the last physical evidence of their relationship.

On their second date, Frank had suggested mushroom foraging. It was morel season in Missouri. He knew a great spot. In advance of the date, Sam drug Timothy with her to LuLu Lemon because she was convinced she needed something new to wear. "Something that says, sporty, but super cute," she explained to Timothy.

She settled on a cute skirt with shorts underneath and a fitted short-sleeve top. Unfortunately, this was the absolute worst outfit for the activity of wandering around in the thick, overgrown woods Frank found for them to explore. By the time they were done, her legs looked like a half a dozen cats used them as their scratching post. But she didn't care. They found exactly two morel mushrooms, which she told Frank to take home to his kids. And they shared about a dozen kisses under the canopy of the forest.

Former boy scout Frank was much more prepared for the outing, and even supplied some of his ex-wife's rubber boots for Sam to wear instead of her less than practical Vans. "There are snacks in the trunk," he explained on the way out to the country. Sam thought it was adorable how prepared Frank was, and how thoughtful it was for him to bring supplies. She tried to overlook the fact that she was wearing another woman's boots for the occasion.

Red flag disguised as chivalry.

The overall loss of Frank still feels heavy on Sam's chest, even weeks after the breakup. A physical manifestation of grief. Sam remembers feeling this in 2001. And what did she do? Well, she got wickedly wasted with the sports reporters, she slept with a traveling cowboy, she dug into her work, and she planned stuff with her family.

Her family, like most, is complicated. Sam's parents are still married, and Jason is the youngest. As the oldest child, Sam has always been independent. Moving to Mill Creek after college was her monumental life move –the thing that was going to propel her into a career of features writing and long-form journalism. She didn't mind being away from her family. Sometimes, she hardly even thought of them. When she moved back to Kansas City after North Carolina, she didn't see them as often as she should have. Later, she was influenced by her ex-husband. Chad never liked Sam's family. He has a big exuberant family, and they always took precedence.

He tolerated Sam's folks, but found them unnecessarily fussy and uppity for his tastes. Sam is pretty sure her parents never loved Chad, but they tried to bring him into the family as much as they could. Conversely, her dad can't shut up about how wonderful Frank is. Just because on a romantic weekend getaway, Frank fixed a few lightbulbs at the lake house, her dad has now dubbed him a handyman hero.

But now, thinking about her family, having no one in her ear with negative thoughts, she has every reason to spend more time with the fam. Maybe she should plan a party! She starts to feel that manic, heavy planning to fix all her life problems energy she felt back in 2001 when she was making the list for Jason's visit.

Slow down.

Ok, a party is too much, but how about we all intentionally plan a trip to the family lake house. Chad hated to go. Frank could never schedule time away to go with her family, although there was that one weekend just the two of them. *That was heaven.* Sam stops the thought spiral she's slipping into. The point is, now no one is holding her back from time at the lake with her family.

She picks up her cell phone and finds her brother's name and picture and hits the call button.

"What's up," Jason answers on the third ring, just as Sam is thinking about what she might say in a voicemail.

"Hey- are you guys planning any trips to the lake house this summer? I want to get some time on my calendar to spend down there with you all," Sam says.

"Yeah, probably, but we don't have any dates set in stone yet. For sure we will be there for the Fourth."

"Oh perfect. I'll pencil that in and we can see if it works out for all of us. Hey- I have a random question for you," Sam realizes she can just ask her brother what he remembers about his visit to Mill Creek.

"Shoot," Jason says.

"So do you remember when you were in college and Mom and Dad would only allow you to go back home or to visit me in Mill Creek?" Sam asks tentatively.

"Um, talk about random," Jason laughs. "Vaguely I do remember visiting you and your roommate…. Dawn, right?"

"Yes, Dawn!" Sam says for some reason really excited to talk to someone about this time in her life, now that she's been visiting it again.

"Ok, so this is weird, but do you remember what we did that week?" Sam bites her lip. "Wasn't that like 20 years ago?" Jason asks. "How the heck am I supposed to remember what I did 20 years ago when I can't even remember if I packed sandwiches in the kids' lunches this morning!"

Sam smiles.

"I know it's weird. I am just…working on something and was trying to remember that week. Anything come to mind?"

Jason pauses and seems to think for a moment.

"I remember beating you at bowling!" he recalls triumphantly.

"Of course," Sam sighs. "But did we do anything else…fun?"

"Yeah, I think we went to the beach. You said it was close and I was used to California beaches, so when we got in the car for two and half hours, I thought you had lost it." Jason laughs.

Sam is so relieved to hear this, she could cry. Maybe she is helping her younger self, or maybe her younger self is helping her? She isn't sure yet.

"Thanks," she says to Jason, flapping her wrists in the air in a fanning motion near her eyes to keep from crying. "That's what I needed to hear."

"Okay, any other completely random memories I can help you reconstruct?" he says with a sarcastic tone.

"Nope, that's all! Have a great night and let me know about the Fourth!"

Well that was interesting.

She's just discovered she has changed the past with her actions in 2001. Because while she has no memory of going to the beach with Jason, he now remembers differently. She chews on the knowledge that she can change the past. I did change the past. *If I go back again, I could really change it.* However, she is about to bite off much more than she can chew.

2001
Mill Creek
A Tennis Court

Sam is holding a tennis ball in her right hand. The hot sun blazes down on her. She squints. A very attractive man with wavy sandy blonde hair, wearing shorts and a polo, bounces a tennis ball on the ground with his racket.

She was down to the last gummy in the bag. She told herself it was her last hurrah in her old life but after this, she absolutely had to live in the present. No more time traveling! But the knowledge that her actions in 2001 do have an impact on her 2024 life make this last trip a little more interesting. Hopefully she doesn't do anything to wipe herself off the map or completely uproot her present-day life.

Sam groans out loud. "Oh fucking hell," she says out loud. She turns to her right and a young boy, probably 11 or 12, gives her a wide eyed stare at her use of bad words. She shrugs.

She knows exactly when and where she is. She is at, or rather, in the middle of the court of the 2001 Mill Creek Tennis Championship

Tournament. And she is not there voluntarily.

A few weeks prior, she had missed an editorial meeting when an interview with a doctor at the hospital for the health story ran too long. When she did return to the newsroom, there was excessive snickering coming out of the sports department area of the newsroom. To be fair, this was nothing out of the ordinary so she returned to her desk.

There was a note from Amy on her computer's keyboard.

"Ed wants to see you when you get back." There was a heart drawn under the text and Amy's signature.

Ed was the managing editor. Nothing good ever came from an "Ed wants to see you when you get back" note in the history of ever.

She looked up at Amy who gave her a pained, "this is out of my control" apologetic smile.

Sam had meekly knocked on his door. He waved her in.

While Sam had been stuck waiting with the angsty PR lady for the tardy urologist to honor their appointment, the newsroom plotted against her. They collectively decided that she, Sam, needed to do a first-person feature story from the perspective of "ball shagger" at the upcoming Mill Creek Tennis Championship Tournament.

Typically, ball shaggers were 11–12-year-old kids who played tennis and wanted the experience of assisting in a more advanced tennis tournament. But someone in the sports department (Sam always suspected it was Loren) suggested that a first-person feature story by Sam would offer a quirky twist on the story. By quirky twist he meant Sam was so uncoordinated she would probably twist her ankle in an attempt to shag any balls rolled her way. Sam was notoriously clumsy. And Loren (or whomever had hate-nominated her for this story) was not wrong that the story would have drama.

"HELLO! BLOODY HELL. ARE YOU A FUCKING IDIOT!" the man with the wavy hair is directing his rage right at her in a British accent.

Sam panics and rolls the ball down the closest painted line of the tennis court. It's apparently not where the ball was supposed to go.

"MOTHER FUCKING ASSININE IDIOT," the angry tennis player says. (Sam thinks he must have studied English at the school of Gordon Ramsey)

The tennis player looks at the referee. "Are you going to let this imbecile interrupt my game with this bullshit?"

The ref blows his whistle and motions for Sam to get off the court. Sam gladly spins on her running shoes and tries to exit the court. Only she goes the wrong way and has to turn around and retrace her path. She feels a million eyes on her and her already hot face flush. She exits the court and nearly crashes into Dawn, who is not at all sweaty. She, in fact, looks like a million bucks wearing a cute pair of flared khaki pants and a button up shirt. Dawn always looked so cool carrying all her camera gear. Her brunette hair is flawless in the stylish "Rachel" cut from the show, *Friends*, that she wears it in.

"Boy, you just bombed that –And I have pics to prove it," Dawn points out the obvious, incredibly amused at the drama she has just witnessed – and apparently has photos of – on the court.

"Can we never speak of this again?" Sam asks humiliated. "I hate them all" she says mimicking the growly voice Dawn had used the night she came home wasted.

"Good thing you have to write about it!"

Sam keeps glaring at Dawn.

"I'm having a great day!" Dawn continues. There have never been this many attractive men in Mill Creek!"

"You have a BOYFRIEND," Sam reminds Dawn of her present-day husband. She adores Dawn's husband, despite his name, which is also Chad, the name of Sam's now ex-husband.

"But HE doesn't have an Australian accent," Dawn drawls in an exaggerated southern accent. Sam knows Dawn's flirting is 2,000 percent harmless. It truly was a fun filled few days with the extremely attractive international visitors. Sam remembers it did cause a fight between Dawn and her Chad, but in the present day, it remains another inside joke between Sam and Dawn. The way they tell it, you would think the Chippendales rolled through town that week. They spent every evening drinking at the Holiday Inn where the players were staying. Dawn had enjoyed flirting with one of the Australian players in particular who'd heard her say, "I have a boyfriend." And took it as a challenge. Little did he know, Dawn was a champion flirter but also loyal and in love with Chad.

Meanwhile Sam had endured the goading of the players for her horrendous ball shagging abilities. Sam remembers no one flirted with her that week.

Sam and Dawn run into Loren who is writing in his reporter's notebook as he walks. Loren low-key has a crush on Dawn, but once again, Dawn is loyal to Chad. She also seems to love torturing Loren with her jabs. "Too bad you didn't make your tennis team in college," she says to Loren who faux punches her in the arm.

"Ow!" she mock yells. "I'm telling Ed about this harassment!" It's hot, and Sam wants to get out of her sweaty Umbro shorts and old t-shirt and into something cute like low slung jeans and a babydoll white top for the Holiday Inn festivities that night. She is putting an outfit together in her head with what she remembers she's seen the past two times she's been in young Sam's bedroom. She suddenly collides into the hot sandy blonde British tennis dude.

This did not happen the first time around in 2001.

He glares at her. She decides this is her chance to correct this man's opinion of her. "Hi," she says and sticks out her hand. "I'm Sam."

He just glares and ignores her outstretched hand. She slowly drops her arm.

"So I'm actually not a ball shagger," she continues.

"You don't say," he retorts in a sarcastic tone but a hella sexy British accent.

"Yeah, so I'm a reporter with the local newspaper. Like the brunette with the camera you guys seem to like" She fires rapidly and points her chin toward Dawn who is standing a few feet away. "Anyhow, the sports guys, the ones covering the games and outcomes, they are jerks. They thought it would be really funny to assign me a story where I try my hand at ball shagging. But they knew I would suck, and it would make a really funny story. However," she pauses to take a breath and realizes she's talking super fast. The rage starts to fade out of his face, and he begins to look a tad amused.

"I'm really sorry it was at the cost of your game." She tries to sound as sincere as possible on the last part. She remembers feeling really bad for all the games she stumbled around trying to make sure the ball was rolling down the correct line. "Just be glad it wasn't a qualifying round," he says to her. "Oh, I'm Spencer by the way." He winks and takes off toward the locker rooms.

Did this just happen? Sam knows for SURE she never got so much as a friendly smile from the players that week in her first go around of this event. Ok, now she's ready to have some real fun. Frank, who? Beau, who? No, it's the Samantha show tonight.

But first, she has a self-deprecating first-person story to file.

****

Sam and Dawn blast Destiny's Child while tearing up their respective rooms, assembling outfits and fussing with makeup and perfume. While Sam originally thought about jeans and a top, she remembers that she might have splurged by now on that fuchsia strapless fitted dress from Express. She originally purchased it for a wedding a few weeks later where she met Jeffrey, the mistake of the century. But Sam hopes young Sam won't mind if the dress makes an early debut.

I'll do something nice for her in the future.

And her memory serves her well. It is hanging in her closet, unlike most of the other items of clothing which apparently live on the floor. She pulls out the store tags and slips on the bold, stretchy fitted polyester dress over her head, shimmying it over her hips and butt. Sam stares in the full length mirror which also doubles as the sliding door to her overflowing closet. Sam's shoulder length dirty blonde hair is pinned up in a sassy high ponytail. She's managed to use every sparkling makeup product young Sam owned to create a glittering masterpiece of over-highlighted makeup. "Going out makeup." they called it back then.

Her shoulders are tan and bare. She's used a sparkly Bath & Body Works lotion to make them shimmer. And the dress hugs every young curve of her body like a glove.

Like a fuchsia polyester 2001 Express dress dream glove.

She's paired the dress with the ever reliable, chunky Steve Madden sandals and silver hoop earrings. She was not able to find anything other than yet another thong in young Sam's underwear drawer, which is really the only downside to this outfit. Although, she has to admit, her cute little 24-year-old butt does look great with no panty lines.

Dawn enters wearing cute white shorts with a strapless bandana top and flip flops. "Too much..." she starts to ask and then takes a look at Sam's getup. "Oh, I see how we are playing tonight, she says with a mischievous tone." With a grin, Sam runs up and throws her arms around her old friend.

"I just love you! You were the best roommate ever!" She realizes her mistake and bites down on her lip.

"Hey!" Dawn says confused. "I'm not going anywhere. What do you mean, you were the best roommate ever?"

Sam stammers, "I… I just mean when you and Chad figure out where you are going to live and all that. I know you won't stay in Mill Creek as long as me." She hopes she has saved this oopsie.

"Well, yeah," Dawn says. I have to tell you, we are already looking at newspapers where we can be together without all the weekend back and forth nonsense." Dawn and Chad were separated by a few hours drive but saw each other every other weekend.

"I know," says Sam. 2001 Sam doesn't know, and is actually clueless in her self-absorbed pity party. But 2024 Sam knows that if this is the tennis tournament weekend, Dawn's departure is not far behind. A photo desk position would open up at Chad's paper, so he would agree to stay as the education reporter, and she would join the newsroom as one of three staff photographers.

"I swear," Dawn remarks, "These days sometimes it seems like you are here with me, like now. And some days, you are on another planet, lady. But it's good to have you here now with me."

"I'm the worst!" Sam says. "I've been a horrible self-absorbed asshole friend. And you have been marvelous, supportive, and only a drunken mess one time!"

They laugh.

"Let's go hit on hot men with accents!" Sam exclaims.

"Woo!" Dawn cheers.

Do people say "woo girls" yet?

****

Sam wakes up expecting to be in her 2024 bed, and slowly realizes she's still in 2001. She sits up and looks around to make sure she's not just imagining this in her hangover haze.

This is not good. This is so not good. What happened?

She lays back down and puts the pillow over her head.

What am I going to do?

What she is going to do is just keep going and hope her "departure" is just delayed. She groggily steps out of young Sam's room feeling like death warmed over.

"Someone is hung over!" Dawn says in a way too cheerful sing-songy voice.

"I need Bojangles," Sam says, without realizing she was even thinking about the fast-food chain restaurant.

"Mmmmmm greasy biscuits, hash browns…" Dawn begins to taunt Sam with items from the menu. This reminds Sam that this version of herself doesn't eat meat. She is still hanging onto her college diet where she claims to be a pescatarian. She's going to have to be careful not to order any chicken tenders while she's here.

Sam cannot eat Bojangles in 2024. For one thing, the mostly southern chain hasn't made it to Kansas City yet. But more important, a greasy biscuit sandwich and hash browns would not metabolize the way her 2001 self used to. She decides to take this hangover and her 24-year-old metabolism to stuff her face and drink her weight in sweet tea. All of the sweet tea.

"I'll drive," Dawn volunteers. She would rather drive than be a passenger with Sam, whose reputation as the worst driver proceeds her. They get in Dawn's Saturn (a popular make of cars for the *Post* news crew) and Dawn immediately turns up the radio when she hears Janet Jackson start up "All for you."

"Remember when they played this last night and we were all

dancing?" Dawn asks Sam. Sam groans at the memory of herself in the fuchsia strapless dress, her shoes off, dancing in the middle of the bar of the Holiday Inn like a girl in her 20's whose biggest worry is paying her utility bills and still having money to go out with. Like a girl who has huge dreams and thinks, this is the beginning of everything. *It is.*

Dawn interrupts her own Janet Jackson concert and turns the radio down again.

"Oh hey," Dawn says. "You got some mail that looked like it might be a wedding invitation. But I have to tell you something…"

Sam instantly knows that Dawn is struggling to tell her that her dear high school friend's Kansas wedding invite was addressed to her and Beau. She decides to give Dawn a day off from broken-heart duty.

"It's ok," Sam interrupts." I saw it on the table before we left."

Train's "Drops of Jupiter" comes on and Sam, who is in one of her thought spirals about being stuck in 2001, decides it's a good time to invent car karaoke a few years early.

Nothing like karaoke to take my mind off the fact I'm literally stuck in the past now.

She turns the radio back up and grabs a hairbrush out of young Sam's purse to use as a microphone. Then she cranks down her window to belt the lyrics. Dawn doesn't need any convincing to participate and joins in, leaning over to share Sam's hairbrush microphone as she drives.

When they pull into the Bojangles parking lot, Destiny's Child's "Survivor" comes on. They look at each other. "Mandatory!" Sam says to Dawn. "We have to," Dawn responds. They proceed to put on a show in the Bojangles parking lot, complete with unchoreographed dance moves and singing into the hairbrush microphone, around the outside of the maroon Saturn. Dawn ends the song by suddenly thrusting herself into the splits in front of her car, throwing her hands up in the air. She was a cheerleader in high school. *Show off.* Sam has no talent other than to throw her own hands up in the air while she kicks her right leg up a little.

The old men seated in the dining room of the restaurant stare at them. It has to be the 2001 Mill Creek hungover performance of the year.

Later, back at their apartment, her hangover now doused in sweet tea, reality really sinks in.

What does this mean? Am I doomed to live the next 23 years over again? And if so, should I make changes to my life?

Obviously she would naturally make little changes, even if she tried not to. Already she's changed many things from last night, including making out with Spencer at the Holiday Inn bar, while the same bartender from her night with the cowboy glared at them. Maybe because she's made so many little changes to the past, she is now doomed to relive it.

Sam realizes the true meaning of "doom" when she feels a familiar cramp in her lower abdomen. In 2017, Sam gave herself the best present a girl with endometriosis who knows she doesn't want children can give herself. She had a hysterectomy. So it's been seven years since she has felt the agonizing pain of her own cramps. She does not want to deal with one of her awful periods. She's already figured out that if she doesn't bow out of 2001, she will have to report to work on Monday. She does not want to have to remember how to be a full-time journalist while dealing with debilitating cramps and constant bathroom visits.

Just what I need to really get back in touch with my 24-year-old body. I really am going to have to buy young Sam new underwear because these thongs are not "it" during period week.

****

It's Monday morning. Ready or not, she and her raging period have to go to work. She dawdles, picking out the perfect outfit for this day – another pair of Gap capri pants and a white Express sweater set with Steve Madden platform slides. She's as ready as she can possibly be.

She gets in her familiar car, which smells faintly of cigarette smoke and is almost as messy as her bedroom, and drives the block to the office. It's almost silly to drive because the office is only a sidewalk block away. Or, you could cut through the parking lot of her apartment complex and between a row of bushes and you'd be in the newsroom parking lot. She would have walked, but she didn't know if she had to drive to any interviews on this day.

The decision to drive proved fortuitous because she did indeed have three interviews on this gloomy Monday. As she walks into the newsroom, everyone is high fiving her for her first-person ball shagging story that ran in Sunday's paper. The picture that Dawn took of her is about as embarrassing as it gets. In it, Sam looks red-faced, her hair damp with sweat, her t-shirt is weirdly tucked into just the back of her Umbro shorts, making it look like a reverse mullet of a shirt. And she's making a face with her mouth partially open at a weird angle.

"I'm never missing another editorial meeting again," she says to Amy who absolutely loved Sam's first-person piece. "That was miserable."

Before she goes anywhere, Sam has to go stare at the wall-sized map of town to get her bearings. She remembers a few things in 2001, like where Rancho is in relation to the newsroom, but it's been 23 years since Sam drove around Mill Creek. And there is no GPS here.

"What's GPS?" Dawn asks, startling Sam, who had no idea she was standing behind her. *Did I say that out loud?*

"Oh, it's this sort of new thing that this company back in Kansas is working on. I think the Navy or something is testing it. It is like a computerized map that you can utilize on a mobile phone," Sam tries to explain Garmin and GPS technology from the future to Dawn in the past.

"Ok, weirdo," Dawn says and walks away.

First on the docket is a trip to Lowes to interview the manager about what to plant this time of year for Friday's Home & Garden. (Always her least favorite story of the week. She used to gripe, "But I don't own a home, nor do I garden!")

She forgets that she had a crush on the manager of Lowes until she is standing in front of him. "Hi," she says when she sees him. He is tall, with short brown hair, a great smile and defined muscles under his uniform.

He looks at her and says, "I saw your story in Sunday's paper. Nice picture." Sam flushes. *So much for flirting with Hot Lowes Guy. Thanks a lot, Dawn.*

"Fertilizer," hot Lowes guy says, getting straight to business. "This time of year, you need to be thinking about fertilizer." Sam remembers why she is there and starts to scribble in her notebook. "Any particular type of fertilizer in July?" she follows up.

Then, she has to meet Dawn at the community theater to take pictures of a dress-rehearsal puppet show for Thursday's Marquee Entertainment story. And she rounds out the day at Sunset Park, where she is tasked with asking total strangers their thoughts on a new development proposal to put in a new shopping center in where the mall destroyed by Hurricane Floyd used to sit.

Sam writes a lot of stories about the recovery from the devastating hurricane, which flooded much of the area in 1999. She knows in 2024, the area is still struggling economically. She also knows, when it rains, the people of Eastern North Carolina still remember Floyd, and then later Matthew in 2016, which wasn't as devastating, but still packed a punch to many in the lower-lying land areas.

On this Monday she stays so busy that she doesn't even have time to loiter at Amy's desk and find out about her weekend. And that's exactly how the rest of the week goes. An entire week.

She tears off the Friday page of her daily affirmation calendar.

Daily affirmations are not helping me here. Will I ever get back to 2024?

It turns out writing feature stories is like riding a bike. You never really forget the process. Sam's job entails a weekly grind of cranking out a health story on Tuesdays, two entertainment stories for Thursdays, a home and garden story on Fridays, religion story on Saturdays, and the big lifestyle piece on Sundays.

"Nice work on the community theater story," Jack doles out an unexpected compliment. "Dawn's photos really made that a nice package."

The community theater was putting on a puppet show to help

children who had been so traumatized by Hurricane Floyd, be a little less afraid of rainstorms. The pictures from under the table where volunteer actors hid their bodies, with their arms stretched up to create the magical illusion of a puppet world are quite clever. The puppets are made of vibrantly colored felt that really pop in the photos.

As much as I'm stressing out about getting back to 2024, at least I'm enjoying my work. I forgot how enjoyable and satisfying it is to be a reporter. This is an absolute blast. From the past? In the past? But why did I not return to 2024?

****

Two weeks pass, and as much as she hates to admit it, Sam is beginning to accept her fate.

What other choice do I have?

And since she's apparently not going anywhere anytime soon, she needs to start strategizing what she is going to do when she "meets" Jeffrey at Louise's wedding. It's only a few days away.

On one hand, Jeffrey was the absolute worst. He was a liar and emotionally abusive. On the other hand, their seven-year relationship shaped who Sam became. And the timing of the end of their relationship coincided with her meeting Chad. 46-year-old Sam thinks she really didn't take any time to grieve or process that breakup.

Regardless, meeting Jeffrey feels like it's about to be another Canon event that Sam should not avoid. What she does in that meeting could mean a total shift in her future life. The decisions she needs to make feel daunting.

Suddenly Sam realizes she has not thought of Frank once in the past week. Not even for a minute.

Well that's something.

She did see Beau's car once. She slowly lifted her middle finger and glared as she passed him.

This almost makes my predicament worth it. Almost.

She wonders if that happened in her first go-around and somehow thinks it did not. She believes a more accurate response from young Sam would have been tears and a spiral into despair.

The same afternoon Sam sees Beau driving around Mill Creek, she returns to the apartment. Something is wrong. Where their living room should be, all she sees is beige nylon fabric. There is just enough room for her to squeeze by what she knows from memory is a tent, and down the hall, past the humming air conditioning unit to her room where she finds an unbothered Dawn eating from a pizza box on Sam's bed.

Oh boy. This is almost as iconic as drunk Dawn the night Beau broke my heart.

"Oh hey," Dawn says with a mouthful of crust. "I bought a tent." With her mouth full, it sounds more like, "I want a mint."

"I see that," Sam says, amused to experience this treasured memory for a second time. "Let me guess. You tried to put it together in the living room and now it's stuck."

"How did you know?" Dawn asks wide-eyed. *I remember.*
"Move over," Sam says as she joins Dawn on her Laura Ashley bedsheets and takes a slice of pizza from the box. "Remind me why you are eating this pizza in my room.

"I don't have a TV in my room," Dawn says, pointing at Sam's small VCR/ television combo she has tuned to MTV's *Real World*. "Duh."

And even though Sam knows the answer to this question, she asks anyway, "What are you doing with a tent?"

"I'll have you know it was on a major sale. Chad and I are going camping this weekend when you go back to Kansas. Neither of us had a tent, so I picked this one up."

"Ok," says Sam, "But that doesn't explain the entirety of our living room being .... tent."

Dawn shrugs. "I obviously had to make sure it was ready for our trip. I just underestimated its size! Things just got a little out of control so I was waiting for you to come home and help me out."

"I love it when you do something unhinged," Sam says without thinking.

"Unhinged?" Dawn asks squinting her eyes. Sam realizes once again she's used a term that is not heard in 2001.

"Uh, yeah, I heard a kid say that at ball shagging class and thought it was a new thing," Sam lies again.

"You've got to stop repeating these weird things kids say. They are not setting trends." Dawn doesn't even try to hide the bossy tone.

****

Before Sam can travel to Kansas for a wedding where she meets Jeffrey, she has to file all her stories. That's just the rule. She can tell Jack is a little nervous that she won't complete her stories for Saturday, Sunday, and Monday before she leaves town. She remembers being stressed about these stories the first time around, and is surprised that she is equally as stressed this second time around. Deadlines are rough, even when you have the assistance of a little time travel.

A news tip came in the week before, giving Sam a fantastic Sunday story. Sam started at the *Post* about nine months after the flood from Hurricane Floyd, but hurricane recovery has dominated the paper's news coverage since she arrived. Even though Mill Creek and surrounding areas were two hours inland, the storm sat over the area and the rain wouldn't let up. Sam never turns down a Floyd story.

The town of East Valley, NC was given to freed slaves in the 1800s. However, they so "kindly" gave these folks a 100-year flood plain. As if they hadn't been through enough. During Floyd, East Valley sat under water for ten days. Sam is reminded of Hurricane Katrina and the people of New Orleans in the horrific Super Dome apocalyptic nightmare. *That's still going to devastate all those people.* Sam's brain finds it baffling to be reminded of things that haven't happened yet.

The paper's photo archives include a ton of aerial shots of the town taken from helicopters by the head photographer, Dawn's boss at *The Post*. The pictures show an absolute drowning of the tiny 2,000-person town. It was so horrific; caskets came out of graves and family members had to re-bury their dead. Absolutely every home in East Valley was destroyed in the waters of Floyd when the Tar River rose above its banks, over the levy, and washed out the tiny town. The levy that was supposed to keep the people of East Valley safe failed them, almost as much as the system that gave them the town to begin with. Every East Valley resident who survived the flood had a story to tell about that awful night in September of 1999.

This week, Sam got a news tip that East Valley resident, Patricia Pitt's Floyd story had an unexpected happy ending. The night of the flood, she bravely drove her three children out of East Valley as the water rose. The flood water felt Biblical to Patricia, as it washed away the only place that had been her home for her entire life. She also lost her only source of income that night when Floyd took out a shopping center in neighboring Mill Creek, where she worked.

But Patricia has a new job now. She is employed by the city of East Valley, which is in the process of building a brand-new town hall. And, on top of the new job, she also has a new home. Habitat for Humanity has been busy building as many new homes as possible.

What makes Patricia's story even more wonderful is that the single mom of three has met a volunteer who came down from Virginia. His name is, ironically, Floyd. He felt compelled to come help in East Valley after the hurricane, and they met and fell in love. They are getting married!

****

Sam and Dawn crowd into the tiny home that smells of fresh drywall and paint to interview and photograph Patricia and Floyd enjoying their new home. Sam's 2024 self recognizes this is a public relations story for Habitat for Humanity, but it's still such a good one.

As a young reporter she never thought about the business side of the news. In fact, the entire advertising department was somehow considered beneath her. Now, with more experience, she thinks her younger self was self-absorbed and ridiculous.

How did I think the paper made money to pay me?

She now finds it interesting to consider the business perspective of the content she created.

Even though she's been back in 2001 for a few weeks now, and been in more than a few peoples' homes, she's also reminded of how weird it is to be a small-town reporter and just march into people's homes to ask them personal questions while a photographer takes pictures.

Floyd is helping Patricia's oldest son with his math homework at the new kitchen table. Patricia shows off her brand-new kitchen appliances. She turns on and off the garbage disposal proudly. Sam thinks no one has ever been more deserving than Patricia of this modern convenience.

The rich aroma of some sort of stew emanates from the stovetop.

"Can I have you, maybe stir what you are making in that pot?" Dawn asks, seeing an opportunity for a great photo.

Patricia grabs a wooden spoon and begins stirring while Dawn snaps pictures with her digital camera. To Patricia and her two younger children's delight, Dawn is able to turn the camera's screen toward them and show them the pictures she's taking immediately after taking them. Digital photos are so novel in 2001. The entire family stares in awe of the new technology and apparently love seeing their photos on the tiny screen.

Wait until they see smart phones.

"What was it like the night of Floyd?" Sam asks. She is holding her reporter's notebook in one hand and a pen in the other, ready to scribble notes furiously in the serial killer handwriting that only she can decipher.

"I was so scared, and I was praying to Jesus. My kids were in the backseat wailing, and that rain just kept coming down. We was low on gas, and I didn't know if our little car could make it through the high water," Patricia recounts the nightmare of a memory.

"What role did your faith play that night," Sam asks a follow up question.

"I just knew that God sent that flood, and He was also going to wrap his love around me and my kids and get us up out of there. I just had to believe that or I wouldn't have made it," she says, her voice cracking.

Sam nods. Meanwhile, Dawn is taking pictures of the oldest son with his new stepfather to-be.

"Can you tell me about your new job," Sam continues.

"Oh yes! I am so grateful. I'm in charge of flood relief management and am going to be a liaison between the community and FEMA," Patricia says proudly.

There has been a lot of strife between FEMA and the displaced residents of East Valley, and other community members whose homes were destroyed. The push and pull of federal funding and difficulties with communication between the agency and the residents have caused rumors to run rampant about false timelines. The people of East Valley are getting fed up with FEMA in 2001. There is also a lot of crime in the tiny city of FEMA trailers where residents wait for a new home and flood relief.

"What do you see as the greatest challenge ahead for you in the role?"

Sam follows up her last question.

"I think the people of East Valley are tired of waiting around and hearing rumors of rebuilding, with no action. So, I think I have a bit of a battle to help correct some of the information that's out there," Patricia answers. Sam smiles and thinks that FEMA would really like the statement from a PR perspective.

"And when is the wedding?" Sam asks.

"We're going for September 15," Patricia says proudly. "Because that's two years to the day of Floyd, and I want to create a new memory with a new Floyd for that day."

Ok, that is adorable.

Sam turns to Floyd and asks the question she has to ask, "How do you feel about sharing a name with the hurricane that took your fiancé's home and livelihood?"

"Well," Floyd says. His voice is somehow both soft and deep. Sam has to strain over the noise of the other children playing in the small living room to hear Floyd. "When they were talking about that hurricane on the news, I couldn't believe it had my name. But then, maybe I wouldn't have paid attention so much as to the news about it and maybe I wouldn't have wanted to come down here and help if it didn't have my name on it."

Sam knows a little something about fate and things meant to be.

Sam and Dawn say their goodbyes to the happy family, and return to the newsroom where Dawn edits the photos in the archaic version of Adobe Photoshop and Sam works on the story in Word on her giant computer. She frequently has to ask Amy for help using said device now that she's been back in 2001. Amy never judges her. She just looks at her with pity and thinks she's spacey due to the breakup. Meanwhile, Jack 100 percent judges her from his adjacent cubicle every time.

Sam lets Jack know that her story is saved in the drive. She thinks about how in 2024, she'd just email him the story, but they don't have work email accounts yet. Sam just has a Hotmail account for personal use. Jack thanks her and tells her to have a great trip.

"Don't get too drunk," he chides. He knows the wedding is dry and he's just goading her.

With the deadline met, Sam can now focus on the bigger obstacle in her future: Jeffrey.

*****

The night before the Kansas City trip Sam melts down. In fact, her meltdown manifests itself the exact same way it did the first time around, but for completely different reasons. While packing, Sam finds a spot on the strapless Express dress. She vaguely remembers this happening before, even though in her first timeline, she hadn't worn the dress out to party with the tennis players. And that time, she put all of her broken hearted Beau angst into the fit she threw.

Sam has never shared this with anyone, but the first time she attended the wedding, she brought a bottle of Xanax her doctor prescribed after her breakup with Beau. She took one of the calming pills just before the rehearsal dinner, and another one before the wedding. Then she drank on top of it when she and Jeffrey snuck out to find a bar. You are absolutely not supposed to drink with Xanax. This is another thing Sam is not proud of. It's also not something she plans on repeating. She has seen this bottle in Sam's bathroom cabinet since she's been back this time. She's thought about sending its contents down the toilet like the sim card, but regardless, she will not be bringing that bottle with her. She needs to have all her wits about her when she meets Jeffrey.

This time, her pre wedding travel stress is not about going to a wedding single and heartbroken, but about walking headfirst back into that toxic relationship. Of course, she can't express any of that to Dawn, so she just unravels over the spot on the dress. It becomes the focus of all her anxiety going into the weekend.

"What am I going to do?" she asks dramatically.

"Are you really this upset about a little spot on your dress?" Dawn asks, truly puzzled. She would never be this upset about an item of clothing. Then again, she didn't spend a good chunk of her paycheck on said dress.

"Yes. Yes I am. It's a very important dress for the dress rehearsal night. And I spent $46 on it, which as you know is a fortune!" Sam bellows, putting her head in her hands. She can't help but think the same polyester dress would cost $89 in 2024's economy.

Dawn can't argue with $46. It is a lot of money to spend on a single item of clothing at their salary. Not long after they met, Dawn and Sam figured out they both earned the same amount.

"Well I guess we are going to the mall then," Dawn says matter of fact. "Let's go, sunshine!"

Sam grabs the stained dress and follows Dawn out the front door of their apartment, like an obedient child.
"But I already wore it the night we hung out with the tennis players,"

Sam whines. "They'll never take it back."

"Please, leave this to me." Dawn says with more confidence than Sam thinks the situation merits.

This is a different mall than the one that was destroyed in Floyd. It's still very much standing and is a place to be seen in Mill Creek. Once inside, Sam allows herself to be amused at how so very 2001 it feels. There is that Nokia kiosk and the guy trying to sell cell phones. They walk past Hot Topic and American Eagle. They actually have to dodge people in their journey because so many people are at the mall. Dawn walks into Express with the confidence of the Queen of England, *who is still alive now*. She marches her cute little Rachel haircut up to the first associate she sees and puts on what Sam can only describe as an Oscar winning performance.

Somehow, Dawn convinces the sales associate to exchange the dress (without tags or a receipt) for a spot-free duplicate. She lays out a story where Sam is going to a wedding back in Kansas where her ex-boyfriend will be. She has to make him regret dumping her. The sales associate turns out to be a real girls' girl and finds a way to break all the rules and process the exchange. They walk out with a brand new fuchsia polyester strapless dress.

Sam hugs Dawn. "You saved my whole trip!"

"I know. You're welcome," Dawn replies. "Let's get a pretzel before we leave the mall."

"The pretzel is on me," Sam says.

"Oh, then can we get ice cream too?" Dawn asks.

2001

Airport | Raleigh Durham

As Sam has already painfully experienced in her short time as a time traveler, there is no Uber in 2001. It's not like she could afford it if there was, so Sam drives herself to the airport using directions she wrote down and parks her Audi in a park and ride lot. She hops on a shuttle to the terminal. She has a physical ticket that was sent via U.S. Mail to her. She obviously has no phone entertainment and is preparing herself to "raw dog" the flight, as they say back in 2024 when you flew without any tech to watch. Funny, she's already thinking of 2024 as a far away place.

She breezes through security just a few months before 9/11 would forever change air travel. It is incredibly weird not to take off her shoes or remove her liquids from her bag. And there seems to be less yelling from the TSA people than she's used to in 2024.

Once in the terminal, she grabs a sandwich from a Jersey Mike's near her gate. She stops in the gift shop to pick up a magazine to read, in awe at all the options.

I am looking at a graveyard of publications that no longer exist in 2024.

She picks up a copy of *Jane*, her favorite magazine from that time. *Oh how I've missed you, Jane!*

She devours the publication on her flight, then leans back and enjoys the extra room (It's true that airplane cabins have gotten tighter since 2001.) The interior of the airplane looks so old to Sam. There are still little pull-out ash trays in the seats, despite the fact that smoking on planes is banned by 2001. A flight attendant comes by to take her drink order, a Diet Coke.

And before she knows it, she is wheels-down at MCI airport in Kansas City. Sam grabs her suitcase from the overhead compartment and heads down the jetway to the old airport terminal. She is deep in thought about what to do about her pending Jeffrey encounter when she looks up and sees Frank's son. Her mind tries to remedy what she is seeing, and what she knows is reality.

It can't be Frank's son. He's not even born yet. She freezes.

It's not Frank's son. It's Frank. It's young Frank. Oh my god. It's Frank!

She locks eyes with her baby-faced ex-boyfriend. He has less piercings than when they first meet…met? He gives her a friendly smile. She is a stranger to this man. She shouldn't be shocked to see him. She remembers before the railroad he worked for the airline. And here he is.

"Hi," she stammers, her mind racing. *He is so young!*

"Hello," he says. "Can I help you?" he asks politely in a customer service voice she's never heard him use before.

"How are you?" The words tumble out of her mouth. She truly cannot help herself.

Frank looks confused and slightly terrified.

"Do I know you?" he asks with a nervous laugh. Sam is much more attracted to the 47-year-old version of Frank. He looks like a child in 2001.

Not yet.

"Um, not really," Sam swallows. "I know your…" She tries to remember if he was married yet in July of 2001 and quickly looks at his left hand to see if there is a band. When she spots it, she finishes her sentence, "wife."

His face changes and he lights up, which instantly shatters Sam's already broken heart just a little bit more. "Oh, you're a friend of Jessie's!" he exclaims. "It's so nice to meet you. I'm Frank." He extends his hand. It's not quite as rough as she remembers from 2024. She takes it, trying to ignore the spark that travels up her right arm as she touches his skin. She quickly gives his hand a firm shake and drops it.

"Yeah, we um, went to K-State together," Sam gives a probable lie. Then she asks a question she instantly regrets. "How is she doing?"

Frank's green eyes twinkle as he grins. "She's great. Did you know we got married a few weeks ago?"

She doesn't remember the exact timing, but she vaguely remembers it was near her friend Louise's wedding, the very wedding she's in town for, because she always thought the timeline was interesting. He marries her. She meets Jeffrey at a wedding right around the same time. She could have married Jeffrey, but it would have been a colossal mistake. She hardly knew herself enough to find a partner at this age. She could never fathom that Frank and Jessie got married when they were so young, while meanwhile she was still getting her life together.

"Um yeah, um. Congratulations!" She doesn't know what else to say and plasters on a fake smile of her own. "I'm actually in town for a wedding this weekend."

"Yours?" Frank asks earnestly.

He is so cute in his confusion of meeting this stranger. I'm a stranger to him.

"Oh no," Sam laughs. Then she throws out, "That's not for many years." *Why did I say that?*

Frank looks puzzled. "What did you say your name was again?" Sam knows it's probably time to bow out of this awkward encounter before she says something else weird.

"I'm Sam," she says. Then without meaning to she tacks on "Sam I am."

She blushes at that awful reference and tries to recover it. "Sam I am looking for passenger pick up," she says sheepishly.

"Oh," Frank says, "It's there." And he points toward outside, which is only a few feet away from the gate itself. *Good old MCI.* The airport would get a new modern terminal in 2022 but in 2001, it's a relic out of the 1970s.

"Don't get lost," he teases.

"Thanks," Sam says. "Um, tell Jessie I said hi. It was nice to meet you, Frank."

"Nice to meet you too, Sam I am," Frank says.

Sam's cheeks burn as she steps out to the curb, processing what just happened.

I just saw Frank. I saw a young, over-the-moon in-love, newlywed Frank. And now I'm walking right into the dark side of my past where I will meet Jeffrey.

2001
Rehearsal Dinner | Kansas City

Sam zeroes in on Jeffrey at the church during the rehearsal and avoids him. She knows they don't "meet" until the end of the evening, and she's buying herself time. She actually loves seeing Louise and Dan interact. They are seemingly happily married in 2024.

"LouLou!" She exclaims upon seeing her friend for the first time in several years. The girls hug and Sam dotes on her friend the evening before her wedding.

"Can you believe this?" Louise says. "I'm getting married!!!" Sam puts on a giant grin and matches Louise's energy.

"I'm so happy for you!" Sam says, giving her old friend another big hug. She has one eye looking out for Jeffrey and any of his siblings. Jeffrey is Dan's first cousin. Louise was excited when they started dating in 2001 because it meant that in some ways, Sam was a part of Louise's new family. Sam did join several gatherings with Louise's family during the time she dated Jeffrey.

In a world where Sam doesn't want to date Jeffrey, Sam avoids him and his family members. She sees his mother grabbing a piece of cake from the dessert table just as Sam is heading that way. Sam turns abruptly and steps into a chair trying to get away from her. The chair makes a loud screeching noise against the floor. At that same moment, her left foot rolls off the footbed of the platform sandal and she nearly topples over. She catches herself on a table but knocks over the small centerpiece arrangement of flowers. People stare at the commotion. His mother is unaware of her presence, which is fairly on brand for her. Sam only momentarily wishes she had that prescription bottle with her. *I can handle this.* But the end of the night marches forward, despite Sam's looming dread.

Before she knows it, she is standing outside the restaurant waiting for Jason to pick her up. She knows he's going to be late because he gets lost. But she still looks for his Jeep, hoping she can wish his sense of direction into getting him to her on time and avoiding this interaction.

But alas, she can time travel, but not fix her brother's lousy directional abilities. Jeffrey approaches her and lights up a cigarette. The first time around, she had been smoking, and the two had bonded over being the only smokers at a dry, Christian midwest wedding.

"Hello," Jeffrey says, looking her up and down. The fuchsia dress is sexy, Sam can't help but think.

Not for you, buddy.

"Hi," Sam tries to stay cool. It is so weird to see him. Maybe even weirder than running into a young Frank at the airport.

No, that was just plain weird, but this is diabolical.

Back in 2024, there is a trend on TikTok that has turned into a little tune about looking for a guy in finance, 6-foot, blue eyes. Young Jeffrey certainly fits that bill. He is tall, blonde, with piercing blue eyes. This Sam is not blinded by his traditional good looks. Now he just looks like a monster to her.

Sam doesn't have to make small talk with him to know he is a new stockbroker for a major finance company. She also knows that he lost that job after 9/11 because they let go of all junior brokers. That's when he impulsively relocated to North Carolina to be with her. This was a move that at the time felt so romantic and feminist – a man relocating for a woman's career. But now Sam sees it as sad, because he's going to love-bomb his way into her life and then spend years tearing her down with his insults and lies.

She closes her eyes and remembers all the fighting, the name calling, and the misery of their relationship.

Sam decides there and then –whenever then is– that she is not going to let young Sam go through that. *Nope, not again.* She's going to learn from her past mistakes.

"How do you know the couple?" Jeffrey asks.

"Friends with the bride since high school," Sam responds in a curt tone hoping to imply she is not interested in chit chat.

"Oh cool," he says.

There is a long pause where she would have normally responded with, "And how do you know the couple?" She does not ask, but instead continues to watch the road.

"I'm Dan's cousin on his mom's side," he answers the unasked question to fill the awkward silence.

Sam just nods, her eyes peeled for any sighting of Jason's Jeep. "Do you live here?" he asks.

The first time around, she had impressed him by telling him she used to, but now she lives in North Carolina where she is a reporter for a daily newspaper. This time she just responds, "No, North Carolina."

He takes a puff of his cigarette. Sam would desperately like to smoke right now and she knows she has a pack in her purse –She's re-addicted herself since she has been stuck in 2001– But there is no way she's giving him an ounce of commonality.

Finally, Jason's silver Jeep turns the corner. Sam waves frantically to him as if he was a soldier coming home from war.

She acknowledges Jeffrey and just says, "My brother. I don't have a car here."

In the first iteration of this interaction, they made plans to hang out during the wedding the next day, and possibly find a bar between the ceremony and reception.

This time, she just says, "Ok. Bye!" then she gets in Jason's Jeep and shuts the door.

"What's with the enthusiastic waving?" Jason asks.

"I was just really excited to see you," Sam says.

 "Says you never," Jason responds.
"Well, I thought you were really lost, so it was a relief," Sam says.

"Yeah, I did get turned around out here," he mumbles, referring to the small suburb south of Kansas City where the dinner was held.

"I know," Sam says.

Jason looks at her then turns up his radio. Nelly Furtado is playing and Sam leans back in her seat and takes a deep breath. His jeep smells like the tree air freshener dangling from the rearview mirror and AXE body spray.

Little does she know the changes she has just made to her entire life at this moment.

2001
A Wedding Venue | Kansas

The next day, the wedding is absolutely beautiful. Sam wears a long purple bridesmaid dress, a nod to Louise's great love of Kansas State University. The bride is stunning in her simple A-line gown from David's Bridal. The groom cries. The father-of-the-bride cries. Sam manages not to cry. It all goes off without a hitch.

At the reception, Sam avoids Jeffrey like the plague. She can tell he wants to talk to her again. To be fair, there aren't that many single women at this wedding.

The first time Sam wore the purple gown, the two had snuck off giggling to find a bar. And of course, there was the Xanax that gave her a good baseline calm so she wouldn't think about her ex-boyfriend named with her on the wedding invite. Then, after downing some vodka cranberries they returned to the wedding and tore up the dance floor. Louise and Dan's families had given smiles of approval, and there was a lot of whispering about the two.

This time, sober Sam sticks with her parents, who are also guests at the wedding.

"Don't you want to go dance?" her mom asks as the dreaded Chicken Dance song starts playing. Her mom has already expressed confusion as to why Sam isn't hanging out with the other young adults she knows at the wedding.

"Why would I when I have the best company right here," Sam says. Her mom returns a perplexed look of disbelief. It really is nice to spend this time with her younger parents. They aren't much older than she is in 2024, which is one of the biggest mind-blowing circumstances of her time travel to date. Her original 24-year-old self would have rather died than spend the dry wedding reception with her parents.

The Macarena starts playing and Sam lets out an audible groan. "This song is so played out," Sam says.

Her mom gives her another confused look. "It is?"

"I mean, I just meant it's such a silly song that gets played a lot at weddings," Sam tries to recover her blunder.

"Do you attend a lot of weddings in North Carolina?" her dad asks. Her parents are very intrigued by her life on the east coast. They've visited her once since she moved there. Her dad cornered Rob, the sports editor, to get his thoughts on college football trends. She let that happen. A little dad time was good for Rob, Sam thought at the time. Her mom couldn't stop talking about how beautiful Rita was.

"She's kind of exotic, don't you think?" her mom had commented.

Back at the wedding, Sam defends her statement. "No, I'm just very up on wedding trends." She smiles. "I did a lifestyle story on wedding trends this summer." She did not, in fact, write a story on wedding trends. But, maybe she should put it down as a story idea to pitch to Jack. Maybe she could find an angle to make it as a home and garden story somehow.

A DIY outdoor wedding, perhaps.

Her dad changes the subject to tell them about a conversation he had while in the buffet line about a lake house that a family friend just purchased.

"Wouldn't that be fun," he nudges her mom. "Our own place down at the lake!" He has a whimsical look in his eyes.

Sam wants to tell them that they do buy a house at the Lake of the Ozarks. She wants to say it is her favorite place to spend time with them. She wants to tell them about all the decisions she has made sitting on the porch swing down at their dock, including the decision to end her marriage when she went down alone during COVID. But instead, she just smiles.

"It would be a ton of fun. Maybe you could even get a boat," she agrees.

"Up next, we have the BOUQUET TOSS," the DJ rumbles into the microphone. "I need all the SINGLE LADIES on the dance floor!"

Her parents look at her. She feels her face flush, and she's not even drinking wine. *There is no avoiding this. Everyone knows I'm single.*

For a second, she thinks about Frank and their awkward run in, the day before at the airport. They never attended any weddings together, so it's easy to put him out of her mind.

She rolls her eyes and pushes back her chair to make her way to the dance floor.

"Duck," her dad says to her. "I don't want to pay for a wedding in the near future." Her mother punches his shoulder. "John!" she says, "Let Sam enjoy the moment."

Sam leaves her parents to squabble about paying for an imaginary wedding, which Sam now wonders will ever take place?

She catches the bouquet.

Of course she does.

She can almost hear Dawn's laughter at the absurdity of her catching the bouquet without a man currently in her life. Everyone congratulates her.

To her horror, as soon as she returns to her seat, clutching the bouquet, Jeffrey walks over towards their table. Sam avoids eye-contact until she can no longer.

"Hello," he says to their table. Her parents give a warm greeting and her dad sticks out his hand to shake Jeffrey's. Jeffrey introduces himself as Dan's cousin, and throws in that he's a stockbroker, probably hoping to get her Dad's business.

"I met Sam last night at the rehearsal dinner," Jeffrey says, bringing the conversation around to her.

"Yeah, Jason got lost and was late, surprise, surprise," Sam says as her parents chuckle.

Jeffrey doesn't take the hint that she is absolutely not interested in talking to him.

"Well, now that you've caught the bouquet, would you like to dance?" he asks. When a Man Loves a Woman is playing and all the couples are swaying on the dance floor.

"I'm good," Sam says curtly.

Her mom gives her a look. "Sam, you should dance," she encourages.

"No, I'm really good," Sam says, trying to sound resolute in her decision not to dance with her toxic ex-boyfriend from another timeline.

Jeffrey looks uncomfortable and excuses himself. Her mom stares at her, baffled.

"Why were you so rude to that nice, and dare I say, very good looking man?" she asks incredulously.

"He's not that nice of a guy," Sam says truthfully. Then she lies. "I've heard stories from Louise. He's quite the womanizer." She pauses dramatically and lowers her voice. "And, he smokes!" Sam hopes that last detail will get her mom off her back. She's managed to hide her own disgusting habit from them for all these years. Her parents loathe smoking. They complained everywhere they went in North Carolina about how there was just so much smoke. "Well, it is a tobacco growing state," Sam had said at the time.

"I see," her mom says with pursed lips, as she turns back to look at Jeffrey again.

"Mom, don't stare! He'll know we are talking about him," Sam says, her tone conveying just a little bit of panic. This time, her mom rolls her eyes.

Later that evening, Sam is in her childhood home with her parents. In the other timeline, Jeffrey took her out on a date after the wedding. They closed down the bars in Kansas City's Westport entertainment district, and he gave her a very passionate kiss in the driveway when he dropped her off. Sam has never been happier to stay in and play Boggle with her parents.

*****

The next day, her mom drops her off at the airport with some tears. Sam is carrying what she now mentally calls her "bouquet of shame." She feels weird traveling with it, but she also couldn't bear trashing it. She knows how expensive the bridal bouquets are, even in 2001.

She does not see young Frank again, and for that she's grateful.

2001

Mill Creek, NC

When Sam gets home, Dawn wants a full download of the wedding, so she suggests dinner at Rancho. Sam wants to hear all about Dawn's big camping trip with Chad and whether or not the tent which Sam and Dawn gallantly wrestled back into its packaging, held up for actual camping. Over margaritas, Sam fills Dawn in on all the gory details of the wedding, notably it being dry, and the dude who unsuccessfully hit on her.

"I still don't understand why you didn't want to flirt back," Dawn says, "It seems harmless to me. I mean you hooked up with that cowboy… AT OUR APARTMENT."

Dawn wasn't buying Sam's "I got a bad vibe," excuse for not engaging with Jeffrey. Clearly Sam has made questionable decisions regarding men in the past.

"Hey, you were out of town!" Sam responds defensively to the jab about bringing the cowboy back to their place. Then she softens her tone, "But no, it was not the smartest thing I've done in recent months."

"No, but at least you weren't murdered," Dawn says matter-of-factly.

In another timeline, Dawn and Sam had this same dinner, where Sam dominated the conversation with 'Jeffrey this and Jeffrey that.' Jeffrey would have already been planning his first visit to Mill Creek the following weekend. The man moved fast.

"I have to tell you something," Dawn says, her tone growing more solemn and almost sober sounding.

Sam knows what Dawn is going to tell her. Dawn is going to tell her about the photo position opening up at Chad's paper, and that they didn't mean for it to happen so quickly. She's going to offer to pay her share of the rent for the duration of their lease. And the two of them are going to cry.

This Sam, who has already experienced this sadness, wants to help her friend break the news to her, so she inserts the first joke that comes to her mind.

"While I was gone, you hooked up with a cowboy in our apartment?" she says grinning, remembering when she actually had that reverse conversation with Dawn the Sunday night she returned. "Or, you are running away to Australia with a tennis player?"

Dawn laughs. "Nope. Nothing like that. When I rolled back into town this afternoon, someone was sitting on the steps leading up to our apartment."

"Someone?" Sam asks. She's genuinely confused. It takes a lot to surprise Sam, who is reliving her life, and almost always sees every move coming.

"Yes," Dawn says slowly. She picks up a chip and dabs it in the salsa. "Someone I don't think you would want to see…"

"Loren?" Sam says, thinking of the only person she vaguely dislikes from the newsroom.

"No, not Loren," Dawn says and bites into the chip. It seems to take her three business days to chew and swallow the bite before she continues. "Beau."

Dawn just drops the name on the table like it's one of the sizzling hot fajita skillets coming out of the kitchen.

Sam's eyes widen. She takes a big drink of her margarita. Meanwhile, she's processing this information and how to react. This version of Sam doesn't care at all about Beau. Now if Frank had come waltzing up to their apartment, that would be weird, but that would also be harder for Sam to downplay. Still she knows the Sam who Dawn expects her to be, would probably lose it after learning Beau stopped by their apartment. She's not that Sam. In fact, she's not sure what version of Sam she is at this moment.

"What did he want?" Sam asks cooly. Dawn cocks her head at Sam's unexpected cool, collected demeanor.

"To know if you were home," Dawn continues, still looking at her cautiously as if she's afraid Sam is a ticking time bomb who will blow at any minute. "I obviously told him you were in Kansas for a wedding."

"What did he say to that?" Sam asks.

"He wanted to know when you'd be back."

Sam thinks about this. It had to be a result of her making a monumental shift in her future by not entertaining Jeffrey's interest. She just totally didn't see it coming.

"And you said…" Sam digs.

"I said I wasn't sure because I just got back from camping with Chad and I hadn't spoken to you," Dawn answers matter-of-factly. "He said he'd try to call you at work tomorrow."

"Oh my…" Sam responds, imagining Jack having to listen to an awkward conversation between her and the former intern.

"Yeah," says Dawn, taking a sip of her own drink. "And since you don't seem to be falling apart over this news, I have one more thing…."

She proceeds to tell her what Sam already knows about moving. They cry, hug, then order a second margarita. Sam knows the first time Dawn told her she was moving she was so preoccupied with Jeffrey that she didn't really fully grasp the loss. Now, with many good-byes behind them over the years, Sam is genuinely sad Dawn is leaving.

It's going to be lonely in 2001 without you. And what do I do when Beau calls me at work?

"But we still have one last Sunday story to work on together, and we should do something epic before you leave," Sam says.

"Like what?" Dawn asks.

The memory comes to Sam in a flash. Jeffrey had just left after his first weekend visit, and Sam and Dawn discovered they had something valuable in their possession.

"Brownies."

"What?" Dawn questions.

"We should take that weed that Beau left at our place and turn it into brownies," Sam says, remembering the hilarity that ensued. Sam may or may not have peed her pants in their kitchen laughing the night of the "brownies."

"But we don't even know how to make pot brownies," Dawn pushes back. "And what if that's why Beau came by? He was just coming to get that weed," she adds.

"It's not," Sam says definitively. She knows it's not because if he was coming to claim his bag of shake, he would have done it in the first go around. But she is going to have to think about this whole Beau thing when she's alone because it's almost too much for her to comprehend.

Sam almost says, "Let's Google it," in relation to how to make the brownies, but she stops herself. She's had to self-correct herself from referring to Google more than once since she's been back in 2001. She remembers how they actually got the "recipe."

"We'll ask Chad!" Sam says brightly. "He'll know!" Dawn laughs.

"Yeah, he will, won't he?"

"That's why he's the best boyfriend ever," Sam answered. "You are so lucky, Dawn." Sam means it. Chad is one of the good guys. In 2024 he's a faithful husband and a doting father to their two kids. He's also a blast to hang out with no matter what year it is. If Sam ever makes it back to 2024, she should plan a trip to visit those two and their cute kiddos.

Dawn changes the subject, "So, what are you going to do with that giant bouquet that's shedding purple flowers all over our apartment?"

Sam laughs. "I have no idea. Do you want me to toss it to you when we get back so you can get married next?"

"No way," Dawn says. "I'm too young to get married."

Dawn is the same age as Sam but again, more practical in every way. Of course she knows she's too young to get married. Dawn doesn't marry Chad until they've lived together for nearly five years. *Practical.*

2001
Mill Creek Post Newsroom | NC

Sam is so nervous about Beau calling her at work the next day, that she spells three people's names wrong, and is late to an interview. She's never late.

When she returns, she is flustered, and feeling rushed for deadline for that moment, she forgets about the potentially uncomfortable phone call for a moment. Of course, that's when her desk phone rings. She looks down and sees Beau's mother's name on the caller ID.

Shit.

It's not that she's actually nervous to talk to Beau. She's quite curious as to what he could want. It's just that she's not used to unexpected things happening in this timeline. She picks up the phone.

"Post lifestyle desk. Sam speaking." She tries to sound professional.

There is a pause before Beau's familiar southern drawl. "Hey Sam.

It's Beau."

"Hi Beau," Sam says. "I'm surprised to hear from you." Jack's head jerks up from his work and returns quickly to his screen. Sam can tell he wants the tea, even if that phrase hasn't made it to the lexicon of mainstream vocabulary yet.

"I just wanted to see if you wanted to get a coffee or something and talk," Beau says.

"Talk about…" Sam encourages.

"You know, us, and what happened during spring break. I just wanted to explain myself," Beau says.

Sam knows from her Facebook messages with Beau everything she needs to know about "what happened during spring break." This is her time to shine. To represent an older, wiser, unbothered Sam.

"Actually, no, I'm good. I think it's for the best that we split up. I was having doubts myself," she lies. Jack has stopped typing and is just staring at his screen, clearly tuned into every word. "You probably did me a favor in the long run," she continues.

"Really?" Beau says. "But you were so sad, and you, you yelled at me."

Is he pouting?

"Beau," Sam says in a slightly condescending tone. "I've had a lot of time to think about it, and I just don't think we were a good match. You are so much younger than me."

"A year?" Beau replies with slight indignation.

"It's an important year. You were still in college when I met you,

and I've been a professional gal for over a year now. We're just in…
different places in life. I do wish you the best though!" She knows she
sounds way more cheery than she should, but this turn of events is
just too funny to her.

"Um, yeah, um. Okay," Beau sounds slightly defeated.

"Oh, tell your mom I said hello," Sam says smugly before saying
good-bye and ending the call. Jack's head spins toward her as if it is
on a swivel.

"Was that?" he starts to ask.

"Yeah, it was," Sam says. Then in a moment of clarity she realizes she
can probably use this to her advantage. "Would it be ok if I wrapped
up for the day? I'll finish this story, but I…"

"Yeah, totally," Jack says in an unexpected moment of empathy. "Just
turn in that story and go home and put your feet up or something."

Sam smiles. She knows she shouldn't take advantage of this situation,
but she can't help herself. "Thanks, boss," she says.

Once home, she doesn't put her feet up. That would require finding
room on the couch stacked with Dawn's moving boxes. She has to
ask herself if she'd be able to tell Frank to go kick rocks the way she
told Beau.

Could she have said confidently, "You know what, Frank? I was
actually thinking about how unhealthy our relationship was. I'd even
go as far as to call it a situationship.'"

I deserve someone who loves me back as fiercely as I love him.

If Frank ever called her out of the blue to apologize, she hopes she would be that strong.

Thanks, young Sam for teaching me this lesson.

2001
Sam and Dawn's Apartment | Rocky Mount

Now that she has successfully avoided falling for Jeffrey's charm, Sam has more emotional time to worry about getting back to 2024. And, she has time to wonder why she never went back. In many ways, she's resigned herself to reliving her life over again. With her changed trajectory with Jeffrey, she feels more empowered to make more changes.

If she doesn't date Jeffrey, will she meet her Chad? She's already experiencing evidence of the changes. The chances that she still married Chad seem unlikely, but she still doesn't know the full impact her adjustments to the past will have on her future. So far, she knows she altered the future with her brother's visit to North Carolina. She also knows she did not blow up her cell phone bill because when it arrived a few weeks ago, it was just the normal $19 monthly charge. Then there is the whole Beau calling to apologize thing. That was unexpected.

But, what if she's supposed to do something more important than stop herself from dating her toxic ex-boyfriend. What if she's supposed to stop 9/11 and she's been so self-absorbed, she missed the mission? She wouldn't even know where to begin. Maybe she's supposed to be paying attention to the national news? She thinks about all those people who will tragically lose their lives in just over a month. She wishes she remembers any of their names and could maybe anonymously call them and say, "don't get on that plane," or "don't go to work on Tuesday the 11th."

If only I could be the superhero kind of time traveler!

She sits with that for a while, and actually gets teary about it. She's dreading reliving that awful day.

She knows so many other things about "the future" but so few important details. Like this is when she should invest in Apple stocks or something, right? But she has no idea where to begin and it's not like she can Google it or even Ask Jeeves. And forget about sports betting. She wasn't paying attention to sports in the early 2000s. She was just hanging out with the sports reporters.

She returns to the dreaded thought of, what if she's just stuck in 2001. She thinks about all the years between her current reality and 2024. So much growing to do and life to live.

But why is Dawn somehow just as mature in this past world as she is in her 40's?

Now that she's not going to move in with Jeffrey, the future isn't as certain as it once was. How will she end up back in Kansas City if they don't move there together?

She wishes she had answers. And, she misses her dog.

Dawn has already started packing her belongings for her own move. Sam keeps finding kitchen utensils missing and realizing they have gone into one of the boxes labeled "Dawn's Kitchen Stuff." She's also taking the couch which means Sam needs a new one. In the old timeline she didn't get one for months and just lived her at-home life in her bedroom until Jeffrey moved in. Someone finally gave her and Jeffrey the ugliest floral couch known to man. It seriously looked like it came from someone's grandma's basement. She's not sad she likely won't see that couch again.

The landline rings. It's Jack calling her at home. Despite being back in 2001 for a few weeks, she still manages to jump every time the sound of the landline trills in their apartment.

"Hey, Sam. Sorry to bother you after work, but I've got a story that I think would make a great Sunday piece for you. And, it involves some travel. Ed has already approved it. Think you and Dawn can handle a little road trip?"

Sam smiles. *This is Baby's first business trip!* She and Dawn are going to drive a few hours east to Beaufort, NC, where historians have discovered the remains of an actual pirate ship. The story is about the excavation and recovery of artifacts, but it's also a push to get more state funding for the project. Jack found out about the project because in his free time, he apparently read records from the North Carolina General Assembly, which approved a half million in funds for the project back in February.

Jack's journalism skills always far outweighed mine.

The hope is by getting some press coverage, more funding for the project will open up. For Sam and Dawn, it means an all-expenses paid trip to the beach for a night! Sam can already taste the fried shrimp and hush puppies. She absolutely remembers this trip with

Dawn. They had a wonderful time, although Sam knows she talked Dawn's ear off about Jeffrey's upcoming visit.

That won't be a topic of conversation this go around.

Sam runs to Dawn's room to tell her about the trip. "Ahoy, matey!" Sam says in her best attempts at pirate talk. "For I've got a tale that'll shiver yer timbers! We be headin' to Beaufort to lay our eyes upon the grand wreck of the Queen Anne's Revenge, a treasure of a ship that once sailed the briny deep under the banner of the infamous Blackbeard."

Dawn stares at her.

"You've got to be kidding. Is this for real?"

"Aye, it be fer real," Sam says, continuing the pirate shtick. Then Dawn just starts laughing.

"Arrrrr," she tries her own hand at the pirate-speak. "I guess we be going to Beaufort!" she says in her low growly voice.

The paper is going to pay their mileage as well as put them up in a local motel for the night. They are allotted $25 each for their meals. It is certainly not luxury business travel, but it's exciting nonetheless.

Sam has to drive because Dawn doesn't want to risk anything happening to her car before she moves. Luckily there is a map of North Carolina roads in her glove compartment.

Sam packs the outfit she wore the day she met Beau. It's her most professional attire, and it seems appropriate for a business trip. She also adds in a pair of khaki capri pants, a cotton cami, and a knit sweater in case it's chilly at night. Then, she throws in her Old Navy pajama bottoms and college t-shirt she was wearing when she landed in Dawn's bathtub the night Beau broke up with her. She hesitates and adds in a sports bra, her Umbro's, and running shoes in case she decides to go for a run on the beach or something. She knows she doesn't, but just in case!

Dawn scoffs at Sam's bulging duffel bag.

"We're going for one night, you know," she teases. She, on the other hand, has fit all her personal items in a small backpack.

"It's not like there's not room in the car!" Sam justifies. Dawn shrugs and throws her backpack in the trunk.

"Oh, can we make a rule that you don't smoke in the car on the way down there?" Dawn asks.

It's not an unreasonable request because Dawn doesn't smoke, but something about it rubs Sam the wrong way.

"Sure," Sam says in the same curt tone she used when Jeffrey tried to talk to her at the wedding.

"I wish your car had a CD player," Dawn says.

"Well it doesn't," Sam says snippily. "So we will listen to the radio." Dawn flops back in her seat and begins to mess with the dial.

Something is off. Sam can't put her finger on it, but she doesn't remember any tension between them on this adventure. Maybe when they get to Beaufort, it will be better.

But it's not.

Dawn talks the whole way about the new apartment she and Chad are going to move into together, and how they are planning to decorate it. This reminds Sam that she's losing her couch and she'll be stuck in Mill Creek without Dawn, and this time, without a new distracting love interest.

She's in her head about reliving the next 20 or so years, with no road map, when she quite literally misses an exit.

"I think you were supposed to get off there," Dawn says.

"I know I was supposed to get off there, but I didn't, so I will turn around as soon as I can," Sam says between clenched teeth.

"Sheesh, I'm just trying to help," Dawn snaps back. Then she adds, "That GSP or whatever you were going on about would be pretty helpful right now, wouldn't it."

Sam remembers the time Dawn heard her muttering about GPS in the newsroom. Somehow Dawn's comment really gets to her.

"It's GPS for the record," she corrects Dawn sharply.

After what seems like forever, Sam finds their motel and pulls into the parking lot. She tries to adjust her attitude. They don't have anywhere to be tonight, and it is supposed to be their night of exploration. Tomorrow they will meet with the archeologists who are working to conserve the artifacts, which they hope to display to the public in the future.

"We're here!" she says in a fake chipper tone.

"I can see that," Dawn has had it with her bad attitude and has apparently not had the same little pep talk Sam has just given herself to snap out of it.

The room is nothing to write home about. It's a dingy motel room with a single queen size bed.

"Well, we'll have to request you a rollaway bed," Dawn says matter-of- factly, throwing her backpack on the bed, apparently claiming it.

"Oh will we?" Sam asks, her bad mood returning tenfold. "I would think since I drove, I would get first dibs on the bed."

"We can flip a coin!" Dawn says pragmatically. And even though Sam is pretty sure they had a room with two queens in the first timeline, and she doesn't believe they argued, she knows with absolute certainty she's going to lose the coin toss.

With a deep breath, she calls tails.

Dawn flips the coin. "Heads!" she said with a smug grin.

 "Fine," Sam grumbles. "I'll go ask about the rollaway at the front desk."

The door slams behind her.

If online reviews existed, I would be giving this shithole a one star.

(The night doesn't get any better from there.) They find a local seafood restaurant right on the water, but neither of them has much to say, so the meal is painfully quiet.

In the first timeline, they hit up a local bar for drinks after dinner, then walked down the marina, admiring all the yachts. This time, they sulk back to the dingy motel. Sam can't help but think they are two very salty seamen navigating stormy waters.

The next day, they continue to snap at one another. Dawn even interjects a few questions during the interviews, which really irks Sam. Usually Dawn stays in her lane and focuses on her photos, leaving the questions to Sam. Even the archaeologist seems to pick up on the tension between them because she excuses herself quickly after Sam gives Dawn a death stare. To make matters worse, Sam's back is killing her from the night of sleeping on the springy rollaway bed.

They ride home in absolute silence. No one even sings along to the Usher song they love when it comes on the radio. Five miles outside of town, Sam takes inspiration from the archeologist to do some restoration of her own on their friendship.

"We aren't going anywhere until we talk this out," Sam says with the diplomacy of, well, a pirate.

"Says who?" Dawn laughs, but it's not a friendly laugh.

"Says the ghost of Blackbeard," Sam tries to interject more pirate humor.

Dawn rolls her eyes. "Hardy har har," she says dryly.

"But seriously, I know I've been, well, salty." Sam begins. *When in doubt, just go with your heart and tell the truth.* "Okay, bad Pirate puns aside, the truth of the matter is, I'm not doing well with your move. I'm actually really sad about it."

Dawn's scowl begins to fade. "Then why are you being so mean to me?" *Direct and to the point as always.*

"I don't know," Sam says as she begins to cry. "I think I'm just scared that I'm going to be so lonely without you."

The 46-year-old inside Sam knows herself well enough to know she tends to push the people she loves away when presented with conflict. It's a defense mechanism. She also knows she's been acting like a spoiled brat.

"I'm sorry I've been so awful," she says sincerely. "I just don't want you to go."

And I'm scared that I'm stuck in 2001 and have to relive my entire adult life.

She searches her car for anything to blow her nose with and finds an old napkin.

Dawn is quiet for a minute. "I'm scared too," she finally says. "I'm scared that it won't work out with Chad when we live together, and that this whole thing is a huge mistake."

Sam never knew Dawn was having doubts about her decision to move in with Chad. It's actually so refreshing to know that her friend who seems to have it all together in every timeline, is…human. "You are?"

"Of course I am!"

Dawn doesn't have the benefit of being a time traveler who knows that while things are probably not perfect all the time with Chad, they do work out. Sam wants to tell her right now that in 2024 she's still with Chad and they have two beautiful children, three cats, and a dog. She can't tell her friend these things because, first, Dawn would think she is off her rocker. And in all the time travel movies Sam has seen, the golden rule of time travel is you can't tell anyone you are time traveling.

Sam gives her a reassuring smile. "I just have a really good feeling that everything is going to work out the way it's supposed to. You and Chad are going to be awesome. I really believe it."

"You do?" Dawn is crying now.

"I do," Sam reaches across the console and hugs Dawn tightly, savoring the moment.

*****

She turns in the Sunday piece a day earlier than deadline and Jack stares at her over her cubicle.

"What's this?" Jack says.

"You know…my piece for Sunday."

"Seriously Sam? You've literally never turned in a Sunday story early," he says, the shock evident on his face.

Sam shrugs. "You know what? I'm turning over a new leaf."

****

On Sunday, Sam goes into the newsroom to pick up a copy of the paper. There's no way she's paying a dollar for it in a newspaper box. She wants to see her story about the pirate ship in print. The story is teased on the masthead for page L1 of the lifestyle section.

She opens up the small-town Sunday paper, which is sadly thicker than the *Kansas City Star* in 2024 and finds the Lifestyle section. Multiple advertising inserts fall out and land on the floor.

It is a different time for newspaper advertising.

The pictures Dawn took are spectacular. There are close ups of experts carefully restoring artifacts such as plates, cups, and even a hand-grenade. *Who knew they had those in the 18th century?* There is also a wide-lens shot of a model of the ship under a glass case.

Back at their apartment, shows Dawn the layout. The headline reads "Salvaging the Past: The Restoration of North Carolina's Pirate Ship"

"Sweet! My last Sunday feature with you looks great, even if it almost cost our friendship," she laughs.

"I don't know," Sam says. "I think we needed to have that tiff. It weirdly makes us closer."

****

Later that evening, Sam has a standing date with Amy to watch *Sex & the City* on HBO at Amy's house. This is before on-demand TV and DVRs made it possible to miss a live showing and still catch an episode. Amy and Sam love *Sex & the City*, and Amy has a coveted HBO subscription. While they want to think of themselves as Carrie, they also both know they are probably Miranda in real life. Sam wants to tell Amy about the reboot of the show in 2021. She knows she would love to hear it's still culturally relevant, even if it has been–correctly in Sam's opinion– panned by reviews. Despite the sometimes cringey plotlines, Sam remains loyal to watching her favorite characters.

If I ever return to 2024.

While Sam is at Amy's, Dawn consults with Chad for the brownie "recipe." He tells her it's not really a recipe as much as it is to cook the pot in butter which infuses the THC into the treats. They aren't trying to get fancy, so they use a box of brownie mix for the occasion. They have the shake off from Beau's bag of weed he left at her place when he fled with his dog and his tail between his legs after breaking up with her. They hope it's enough to produce an edible high.

Sam smells the pungent aroma of weed before she's even inside the apartment. She laughs because Dawn is trying to mitigate the smell by placing a rolled up purple towel under the door.

"Nice try, but when the DEA comes, I don't think a towel is going to mask this funk," Sam says upon entering.

Dawn glares at her as she stirs.

"Do you have a better idea, Einstein?"

"Yes. Weed should be legal,"

"That's not likely in our lifetime," Dawn grumbles.

Well not yet at the federal level, but in 2024 we both live in states where it is legal.

When the brownies are out of the oven, they both stare down at the Pyrex full of the potentially trippy treat.

"We should wait for them to cool," Dawn says practically.

"Or. OR, we could burn our tongues off with THC chocolate lava," Sam says.
They debate what they should watch while the brownies kick in. Sam remembers they watched *American Pie* because she had a VHS of it, and it was funny. Chad suggested they should turn on something humorous.

Like so many things from 2001, this movie wouldn't have passed the vibe check in 2024.

They bring their brownies into Sam's bedroom. The only VHS player is attached to her TV. Sitting on blue and yellow floral sheets, they press play, start the movie and dive into the brownies.

"Mmmm," Sam says. "Not too skunky! Good job, Dawn! And thanks, Chad!" She gives Dawn a little side hug.

Since they've both seen the movie many times before, they talk over the beginning of it.

"How long do you think these things take to kick in?" Dawn asks.

"I don't know. What did Chad tell you?" She knows how long dispensary edibles take to kick in, but she's not sure if the homemade stuff is different.

"I forgot to ask," Dawn says giggling. "I was so focused on the whole butter infusion process."

About thirty minutes into the movie (and Sam is internally groaning at the sheer 90's of it all) Dawn says, "do you think we should have another? I'm not feeling anything."

Sam looks at the clock on her nightstand. It's already 10 p.m.

This is so past my 2024 bedtime.
"Uhhh...I don't know. Maybe we should give it another 15?" She can't remember if in their first pot brownie adventure they had seconds before the brownies kicked in. All she remembers is they hit hard and fast when they did kick in.

"Probably a good call," Dawn says. Then she pauses, looks at Sam and says quietly, "Does it make you sad to use the last of Beau's weed?"

Sam stops to think. In her first version of 2001, heartbroken about Beau, but hopeful for things with Jeffrey. She thinks about Frank. It still hurts, but something about deciding not to engage with Jeffrey has freed a piece of her heart. She feels somehow stronger and more empowered. She can't put her finger on it, but she knows she doesn't have the same dagger twisting sensation she did back in March when she started time traveling.

When it comes down to it, Sam has always sought out validation from men in her life, whether it be from the sports guys or Beau. Or, even a random cowboy and hot tennis players. Then there was Jeffrey followed by her ex-husband, Chad, and yes, Frank. Maybe especially Frank. Because as much as she loved him, he never loved her back. Trying to make him love her was death by a thousand cuts. It hurts even more because they were such good friends, and she saw such a future with him. In many ways, it still feels like the loss of her life. But it doesn't matter. He ended it. She'll probably never see him again, and her life is certainly no longer the same as it was before she started popping time travel gummies.

She thinks even though she's stuck in her 24-year-old body and her 2001 life, she's actually thriving on her own self-love. Being back in the past has reminded her she is a talented journalist with amazing friends and family. And probably most important, it has shown her that she is still the tenacious, fearless reporter she was in 2001. Which is probably a good thing because she doesn't see herself going anywhere anytime soon.

"Sam?" Dawn says. "Are you in there?"

She nods as she is remembering how her heart had shattered the night Beau dumped her, and the equal amount of euphoria over his apology phone call days ago. Some things are too ridiculous not to laugh at. "What kind of loser breaks your heart and leaves his bag of weed? I think this is the best idea we've ever had!" Sam finally says.

And they burst into giggles, but the giggles sound strangely far away. Sam reaches out to grab Dawn's hand when all of a sudden her head hits something very hard and cold.

Not again.

2024
Lake of the Ozarks, MO

This time instead of Herbal Essences bottles, there are children's bath toys all around her–and she might be sitting on one. She recognizes the tub and all its toys and knows she's at her family's lake house. She can hear the sounds of her niece and nephews playing what sounds like a game of hide and seek. The shower curtain starts to move and a pink dog nose pokes its way around the curtain where she's apparently hiding.

"*Millie!*" She yells out loud without thinking of the hide and seek game. She is so excited to see her dog. Besides worrying if she'd ever return to 2024, her fears about Millie were at the top of her worry list. Does she still have her beloved rescue dog? And here is Millie licking the tears that are apparently streaming down her face.

Suddenly a small hand opens the shower curtain all the way and a boy of about 5 shouts, "I found Aunt Sammy!" He says "Sammy" with the slightest hint of a lisp. It's her youngest nephew. Now she is full-on crying. She truly thought she was doomed to live her 20's,

30's and half of her 40's all over again, and while the youthful body (despite dealing with a period) was amazing, she really doesn't want to relive all those years.

I really thought I was stuck in the past.

"Why are you crying, Aunt Sammy?" Peter asks her with great concern.

"I'm just so happy you found me," she sniffs and hoists herself out of her hiding spot to grab some toilet paper to blow her nose.

Peter looks at her like she is absolutely nuts and turns and runs out of the room to tell his siblings he's won this game of hide and seek.

Millie is still wagging her tail and sniffing Sam, probably concerned about the emotional outburst as well. She's wearing biker shorts and an oversized unfamiliar Portland, OR t-shirt. *When did I go to Portland?*

Her face is fuller than it was back in 2001. She has some wrinkles around her eyes, and her lips seem thinner, which is a little disappointing.

She's become so accustomed to seeing her 24-year-old face that it's a bit jarring to see her older self in this mirror. She pulls her t-shirt down a little lower from her neck, and sure enough, a delicate flower tattoo peeks out at her.

Well that's different.

She goes downstairs to the kitchen and living area to get her bearings on her current situation. Feeling self-conscious about her parents seeing her new tattoo, she pulls at her shirt, then realizes it's probably not a new development.

Millie trails at her heels.

Her Dad is in the kitchen pouring batter into a waffle maker. "Do you want a waffle, Sam?" He doesn't look up.

"Um," Sam has to think. She is not hungry. "I'm good, but I'll grab some coffee." Sam spies the French press half- full of the fueling liquid she needs to process her new–or is it old– life

"Help yourself. I already gave Millie the dog waffle." The dog waffle is the first waffle out of the waffle maker because it never turns out quite right, but dogs don't care. Her dad invented this tradition when she was a kid and they had a dachshund, who happened to love imperfect waffles.

"I'm sure she appreciated it," Sam says looking around the kitchen. It looks exactly the same as the last time she was at the lake with Frank. She will not think about that right now. Instead, she pours herself the remaining coffee in the carafe.

Her mom is in her "spot" on the screened in porch journaling and reading news articles on her laptop. Sam pulls open the squeaky door from the kitchen. "Hi Mom."

Her mom looks up from her laptop with a concerned look on her face. "Didn't we just say good morning a few minutes ago?"

Sam truly has no idea what she was doing a few minutes ago in 2024 or really anything that has transpired since 2001.

"I just wanted to tell you that I lost hide and seek to Peter," Sam tries to explain her weird second greeting.

"No one can hide from Peter for very long," her mom says about the busy pre-schooler. "Did you get some waffles?

"I'm not hungry." She pulls a wicker chair out from the table to sit next to her mother.

"Are you excited about your big day next Saturday," her mom asks.

Sam plays along. "Um, yeah. Pretty exciting stuff."

"I mean your very own bookstore *is* so exciting."

Sam's heart lurches into her stomach. Good thing she's sitting down.

"Bookstore?" she asks.

Her mom laughs thinking she's joking around. "I know! Who'd have thought we'd have an entrepreneur in the family."

Sam is speechless. She has so many questions but doesn't know how to ask them without looking bat-shit crazy. Luckily, she's been playing this game for many weeks in 2001, but the opposite, where she has the answers but has to ask anyway.

"So, are you guys planning on coming?"

"Of course we're coming! We wouldn't miss the grand opening of Chapters & Cheers for the world!"

Chapters & Cheers was the name of the bookstore Sam and Chad tried to open when COVID came and shut everything down.

Wait a minute! Am I still married to Chad?

"Do you think," she pauses trying to figure out how to ask, "Chad will be there?" she finishes.

"Chad? Who's Chad? Is that someone you are seeing?"

Sam breathes a sigh of relief.

Sam tries not to smile. *Thanks, Mom! Great intel. I'm single and dating. And Chad was never part of my life.*

No Chad. No Marriage. That's a lot to process.

What have I been doing all these years?

She tries another fishing question. "What about Frank?" She holds her breath.

"Frank?" Her mom furrows her brows "Isn't that the guy you met at Jason's show a few years ago? I thought you went on one date with him and it wasn't good. Are you seeing him again?"

"Probably not," Sam says. More to process. So she did meet Frank and even went on a date with him, but apparently not the same date she went on in her original timeline where they fogged up his car windows.

"Are you okay, Sam? You're acting very strange."

"Um yeah, I uh, just couldn't remember," Sam tries to act nonchalant about her absolute ignorance about her entire adult life.

"So I said the date with Frank wasn't good?" Sam can't help herself.

"Yes. You were pretty convinced he wasn't ready to date at all yet. Something about his divorce and his ex-wife," Her mom says. She closes her laptop and really looks at Sam, scrutinizing her. "Sam. I'm worried…"

Sam cuts her off, "Who else do you think will be coming on Saturday?"

"Well, Jason, Kristyn, the kids, I think maybe Louise's parents will be dropping by, and your friends Donna and Sean, right?"

Sam is so thankful to hear she's still friends with Donna and Sean.

"Yeah, totally," she says with more confidence than she feels. "I'm fine. I'm um, going to go down to the dock for a while."

With Millie at her heels, Sam heads Sam gets up with Millie behind her and slowly walks down the deck steps and onto the rock steps leading down to the dock.

So I didn't marry Chad. I'm opening our bookstore, presumably as a solo owner. And, I only went on one date with Frank because he wasn't ready to date. How keen of me to pick up on that. Why didn't the first version of myself figure this out before I got absolutely destroyed with heartbreak? Because maybe this new version of me doesn't need him to like me. Maybe Sam 2.0 has more discretion with her dating life.

She sits on the familiar creaky porch swing. If ever there was a time for a cigarette, it's now. But Sam knows she has to quit the gross habit again now that she's back in the land of no-smoking. The dock sways a little from the wakes of nearby boats. Millie stands at the edge of the dock watching the boats go by, barking when she sees another dog in a boat.

Sam sits there for at least an hour. She's actually pouring sweat because it's so hot down at the dock. It's clearly summer, but is it the fourth of July? She's forgotten how hot she gets as a middle- age woman. Her 24-year-old self didn't sweat to this degree.

She hears the sound of the kids making their way down to the dock. Her brother yells, "Life jackets on, kids!"

Peter, 5, Sophie 8, and Jax, 10 run past her, securing their life jackets to jump off the dock in sequence. They are trailed by Jason, lugging a bag of towels and sunscreen. Millie barks protectively as they jump in.

"Hey Sam," he says when he sees her. "Did you go for a run?"

She grimaces. "Um, no, it's just really hot down here."

"Well get in!" her brother responds to her problem with the obvious solution. Sam is not wearing a swimming suit, nor is she fond of the murky Lake of the Ozarks sludge water. Jax has caught and released some gnarly catfish out of this water. It always grosses her out to think of what is lurking under her when she swims in the lake. Some things don't change when you time travel.

"Are we doing fireworks tonight?" Sam does some fishing of her own for information.

"Not that I know of?" her brother answers with a bit of a question in his voice. "We don't usually do fireworks for Labor Day."

Ahhhh. That answers the question about the date. But there are so many questions left to answer.

"So where is Kristyn?" Sam asks about Jason's wife. Hopefully that's not too out of pocket.

"Up at the house finishing up some work," Jason answers. Kristyn is an employment attorney for a big firm in Kansas City and is always working. "She should be down in a bit. She's going to bring down some sandwiches for lunch, then we might go out on the boat."

Back in the land of wi-fi where you can work anywhere you want.

Sam loves going out on the boat with Jason and fam. The kids' tube behind the boat most of the time, entertaining Aunt Sammy with silly dance moves they pull on the tube.

"I think I'll head up and see if I can help." Sam says as she gets up from the swing, leaving behind a sweat print from her thighs. Her body is heavier than her younger body. It feels weird to be back in it.

"Sounds good," Jason says. "Hey, did you bring a copy of your book for my colleague who wants a signed copy?"

Sam stops in her tracks and turns around to face Jason.

Breathe. Stay calm. Don't act suspicious.

"Oh, maybe, I can't remember. I'll check my stuff," Sam thinks that's a fair answer.

"Cool," he says then, "Jax, don't dive over your brother's head!" Sam slowly walks up to the house.

Book? Is it Two for Smoking?

Everything is so much to take in, and she still has so many more questions.

Back inside, her mom looks at her, "Ew Sam. You are really sweaty. Is it that hot down there?"

"Um yeah, it was steamy…hey, do you happen to have a copy of…" She pauses. It's so surreal to say this. "…my book around somewhere?"

"Yeah," her mom says. "There's a copy on the bookshelf. Remember? You signed it to us?"

"I wasn't sure if it was down here or back at your house," Sam says. If she's not careful with her questions, her family is totally going to send her to a nice long grippy sock vacation at a mental health facility. Actually, as insane as all of this is, it will be a miracle if she doesn't check herself into one. She hopes this version of herself is still taking Prozac and has a therapist.

Since she doesn't know what her book looks like, or even the title, she squats down to get eye level with the bookshelf. Most of the books are children's books, and a few about the lake.

When she sees it, she gasps. She knows it is her book The title is literally, *Sam I Am; A Journalist's Journey to Self-love.*

"Oh my god," she says out loud, removing the book from the bookshelf with shaking hands. She cringes as she remembers the awkward "Sam I am" encounter with young Frank at the airport in 2001.

"Sam? What's wrong with you today? You're acting beyond strange," her mother's voice sounds a million miles away as Sam stares down at her own book.

It's a memoir.

It's not only a memoir, but it's the clue to her "missing" years.

"I'm fine, great," she says, hoping to get her mom off her back. "I'm going to head back to my room and shower. I stink."

In a daze, she stumbles downstairs to the lowest level of the lake house in a daze, and into the room she usually stays in. She's still gripping her book that will hopefully reveal what she's been up to for the past 23 years.

This is too much. I'm back. I wrote a book. I'm opening a bookstore. I never married Chad. Everything is different.

Sam crawls into the comfy bed that she assumes she slept in the night before. One thing about her mom is she stocks the lake house with hotel-grade white sheets that are so soft and crisp. Sam doesn't even care right now that she's gross. She takes a big breath and opens the book.

"To Dawn and Amy for being there for me at my lowest."

Well that is true.

Two and a half hours later–and three check-ins from her mom to make sure she's okay and enquire about when she's going to take a shower– Sam has skimmed her book. She'd really like to dive into it deeper, but she has enough to understand what she's been up to over these years in her new reality.

Sam stayed in North Carolina for a few more years until landing a job reporting for an alt weekly in Portland, OR. At the time, Portland, like Seattle, was able to support two competing alt weeklies, so it must have been very exciting to be there. This Sam has never been to Portland, but she would love to go. She kind of feels like she fits in with the vibe of what she imagines is Portland. And after that, she returned to Kansas City to teach journalism at a local college.
Professor Sam! I guess school will be starting again soon after this

weekend.

For the next 24 hours she tries to not act weird or ask bizarre questions to her family. She's just so glad to be back in 2024. She's found her iPhone and spent some time scrolling back through her social media for more context clues about her new life.

Checking her friend lists on both Facebook and Instagram, she sees many people she doesn't recognize, but a few familiar folks including Donna and Sean. How she ended up meeting them without her bookstore, she doesn't know, but she's so glad. She notes that while there are a dozen news apps, there isn't a single dating app on her phone.

Reconstructing two decades of one's life using a memoir and social media as a guide is daunting, but Sam thinks not as much as reliving all those years. She is so relieved to be out of the past.

The biggest thing she needs to figure out next is where does she live? The chances of her and Millie living in their old apartment seem slim to none. As they are cleaning up the lake house to go home on Monday morning, Sam begins to panic about not knowing where she lives.

Where is home?

She goes through the motions of packing up the car wondering what on earth she's going to do. Finally, she puts Millie in the car, a red VW Beetle, clicks on her phone's maps app, and types "home." An address in Kansas City comes up. She looks down at her keys and sees there is a tag on one of the keys that looks like a house key with 26D written on it. There is also a FOB she doesn't recognize that must open some door. A garage?

So, waving goodbye to her family, she pulls out of the long driveway and heads toward "home." Millie is all the while oblivious to this stress and just happy to be going for a car ride.

Back in Kansas City, she follows the phone's directions to an apartment complex in the River Market, a cute, historic neighborhood just north of downtown.

I've always wanted to live here.

She uses the FOB to open a gate to a parking garage and is thankful the parking spots are labeled with the apartment numbers. She pulls her car into 26D's parking spot, grabs Millie, and her backpack, and heads inside to locate this new apartment. Millie seems to know where they are going. Follow the leader!

All of the excitement of having a new place without ever having to move. Kind of amazing!

She puts the key into the door (hoping this is not the wrong apartment) and opens it up to see her new digs.

Almost everything is new to her except her bedroom set, a hand-me-down from her parents, and a few of the framed pictures from childhood.

Not bad. I have good taste.

Millie circles a few times and makes herself comfortable on a beige dog bed.
At least she recognizes this as home.

She sees some framed articles on the wall from *The Post* that she recognizes, as well as several from the Portland weekly publication that she doesn't. Her book cover is also framed on the wall.

The couch looks inviting after the stressful drive of wondering what she would walk into. She decides a nap is in order, and Millie jumps up on the couch with her, apparently claiming her regular spot.

2024
Kansas City

Sam has figured many of the details of her professional life by reading emails. On Tuesday she drives to the campus labeled "work" in her phone. She thinks she did a somewhat decent job at pretending to be a professor. Maybe she should pick up a book.

Is there a Dummies guide to teaching journalism?

The students are all so interesting and eager to learn. A group of girls is planning to come to her bookstore opening. She's learned from emails that she's dropped her course load down to two classes this semester in order to launch her business. The university is supportive of her endeavors.

She's also learned from email where her store is, and the name of her one and only employee, Dana. The name sounds familiar to her, but she can't place it. After class, she gets in her car and drives to the location she found in the emails.

There it is. It's in a different location than the original Chapters & Cheers. It's nestled away in a neighborhood called Hyde Park, and shares walls with a butcher on one side, and a women's clothing boutique on the other side.

On Tuesday, it's not fully ready to open, but she knows that Dana is supposed to be coming in for a few hours to help her manage inventory and get the shelves stocked.

When the door jingles, Sam is shocked to see the tall, brunette bartender from her favorite bar in her original timeline.

That's how I know her name!

"How can I help this evening," Dana asks, eager to be put to work.

The two of them process inventory, make great progress on stocking, all while talking about the opening on Saturday.

"What should I wear," Sam asks Dana.

"Ooooh great question. I really like that one blue, satin pleated midi skirt you have. One time you wore it to the bar with a Kansas City t-shirt and some sneakers. I remember it looked so good."

So Dana did work at the bar. Interesting that I still found my way to that establishment, since I no longer live nearby.

"Ok, but what if I mixed it up with the shoes," Sam asks. She shows Dana a picture of her recent purchases on her phone's Amazon app. The Steve Madden slinky slide platform sandals are still in the box back at Sam's apartment.

"I just bought these," Sam shows Dana the shoes.

"I think I've seen those before. I want to say my mom had a pair when she was in high school. They're vintage!"

Dana's mom is probably my age.

Sam grins. "Yeah, I used to have a pair back in the day and wore the hell out of them! I thought they might be cute. I can't believe you can still buy them!"

Before she left the lakehouse, Sam had purchased what she called her time traveling souvenir. It was fun to be back in the world of instant gratification via online shopping.

"So, is there someone you would want to bring to the grand opening?" Sam asks Dana.

"Awww that's so nice of you," Dana says with a big smile growing on her face. "I am seeing a really sweet girl. I met her a few weeks ago and she'd totally love the vibe of this place. I'll see if she wants to stop in."

There is a little silence as they break down the boxes they just unpacked.

"What about you," Dana returns the question. "Are you seeing anyone? I've never seen you bring a date to the bar."

"You know," Sam says and takes a deep breath. "I'm really happy with my book and the store right now. I'm not saying I wouldn't date, but it would have to be someone pretty spectacular at this point."

An interesting thing since she's returned to 2024 is she has no desire to contact Frank. She knows they had that one date because her mom told her. She's even found and since deleted his contact info in her phone, just in case she does have a weak moment after dangerous margaritas.

She also knows there is a good chance she has a shot at getting his attention this time around. Yes, she could play it cool and ask for a second date, and if he's not seeing someone else, he'd probably say yes. After all, it wasn't spending time with her he was afraid of, but rather commitment and being vulnerable with his emotions. Then again, why would she do that to herself now? Why would she open herself up to allow an unhealed man to hurt her when she's been given this unique second chance at her life?

"Yeah," Dana sighs. "It's rough out there. I get that."

"Not just that dating sucks," Sam continues. "But I'm also really learning to love myself. Is that cheesy?"

Dana looks at Sam for a beat, almost in awe.

She's really that much younger than Dawn and I were in 2001.

"No, that's so cool. Mad respect for your standards and self-love!"

Sam gets up and grabs two water bottles from the bar. "I think we

should toast to that," she says.
They tap water bottles and Sam says, "To loving yourself more!"

Dana repeats.

****

On Wednesday evening, she is settled in for a night in her "new" apartment with Millie when her phone rings. "Directory Assistance" pops up on her iPhone screen. *What is Directory Assistance?* She answers it and she hears crackling on the other end. Then, a familiar voice, "Hey- buzz me in, bitch!" *Timothy?* She presses a green check that pops up and hears a short buzz and then the line goes dead.

A few minutes later someone knocks on her door to the tune of Shave and a Haircut and then, the door which she apparently didn't deadbolt, swings open. Timothy shows up with a bottle of white wine and a glass Pyrex container. He looks fabulous, as always. He's wearing really tight acid wash jeans that have a slit in the back, under his ass. Only Timothy could pull these jeans off.

"Are you ready for Whinge Wednesday?" Timothy says in a horrible British accent. "Bob's your uncle!"

"What?" Sam is stunned. It's not the first time Timothy has shocked her, but it is the first since she returned from 2001.

"Are you kidding me?" He says the words slowly and loudly as if Sam is hard of hearing. "Whinge. Wednesday?"

Sam is vaguely aware that whinge is the British term, "to whine," but she doesn't have any idea what a Whinge Wednesday is. She takes in the context clues - something any savvy time traveler knows to do. He's holding a bottle of wine. That must be the whinge. It's Wednesday. So Whinge Wednesday.

Sam taps her head as if she's so forgetful. "Oh yes, I had my days confused," Sam says. "Back to school and the whole opening a business thing."

"I know, love, but it's important to keep up your routine!" Timothy sets the wine down and hands her the container that looks like it has some sort of cookies in it.

"I attempted to make the biscuits."

The biscuits?" Sam asks.

"You know…. *the* Ted Lasso biscuits!" In the show, Ted, a transplant to the United Kingdom, learns how to make biscuits, the English term for a cookie served usually with tea.

Not Ted Lasso. That's what I was watching with Frank before we broke up….in a timeline that doesn't exist…

"We are on Season 2, episode 4!" Timothy reminds her.

Of course. The same episode Frank and I were on.

There is nothing else to do but grab two wine glasses and put the biscuits on the coffee table. Millie inspects them, wags her tail and curls up on her bed.

"Let's fire up some Ted!" she says brightly.

****

There are a few consistencies in this reality that interest Sam. Little things like being on the exact same episode of Ted Lasso as she was with Frank. And, major things like the fact that she still has Millie and she drives the same make and model of car, if not the same exact car. In a timeline where everything has shifted, these facts make Sam wonder about the fate of it all. She remembers Patricia Pitt and her harrowing retreat from the flood waters that ultimately led to meeting Floyd.

Fate is fate no matter the timeline. Some things are just meant to be.

****

The week flies by with so much to do at the store. Luckily Sam nearly opened this same store in a past life, so she has an idea of what needs to be done. She feels less confident with the two classes she's teaching. Thank goodness for a strong syllabus as her guide.

Still the morning of the grand opening, Sam feels like she's going to throw up with excitement and nerves. Due to COVID, she never got to have this day, and if she had, she would have shared it with Chad. That would have meant listening to him gripe about all the things that could go wrong. On her own, she keeps a positive attitude. The worst thing that could happen is she could fail, and she won't be any worse off than she was before.

And I won't be any worse off than I was before.

Her parents arrive first. Her dad hands her a bottle of wine.

"Dad, you know I can't serve this at the store," Sam starts to
  protest.

"It's not for the store," he kisses her on the cheek. "It's for you tonight when you get home to celebrate."

"Jason and the kids are going to be a little late," her mom says. "Soccer games."

Louise and Dan arrive next. Louise is carrying purple flowers for Sam.

Of course.

After that, it's a blur of friends, family, students, and even some strangers. She knows from emails that she took out an ad in Kansas City's version of the paper she worked at in Portland.

Donna and Sean bring her a beautiful basket filled with local candles, chocolates made in Kansas City, and of all things, a mirrored disco ball.

"I don't know why, but I just knew you needed to have it!" Donna exclaims. Sam thinks the disco ball will be a fun addition to the bar area in the back.

Thirty minutes later, Jason and the kids enter the store like a tornado wearing soccer gear. Sam shows them where the children's books are. Peter is already asking Jason if he can get a new book from Aunt Sammy's store.

"I don't know, bud. Let's take a look," Jason says. They buy three.

At one point, Sam makes a speech thanking everyone for coming and hoping they love Chapters & Cheers as much as she has loved dreaming of it for years.

Years upon years.

Timothy breezes in with a bottle of tequila and fresh sunflowers. Sam momentarily thinks about how she'll miss the margaritas at Rancho. Then she remembers that she can have dangerous margaritas anytime with Donna and Sean.

"Hey, I meant to ask you the other night: how did those gummies work out for you?"

"Um, well…I mean I got through them all, but I think my gummy days are over."

"Same," Timothy says. "Those gummies made me re-evaluate all my life decisions."

Sam laughs. "You have no idea, Timothy."

She's mid-conversation with a lady whom she has no idea how she knows, but clearly the lady knows her. She's nodding and smiling when Dana taps her on the shoulder.

"Hey, your phone was lighting up and I saw it was a Facetime, so I decided to answer it for you," Dana says in an almost apologetic tone, holding Sam's phone up to show her.

Dawn's 40-something year-old face is on the screen and Sam bites back tears. She takes her phone and quickly slips into the storage closet, blinking back tears. She hasn't spoken to Dawn since she returned to 2024, but all the memories from 2001 are as fresh as if they happened last week.

They did.

"What, you can't make it to Kansas City for your best friends' bookstore launch?"

Dawn laughs. "Yeah, you know I would have if I could, but school started for the kids."

"I'm kidding. Of course coming out here would have been insane, but you know you guys are welcome anytime."

"I have some fans of yours that want to say hi," Dawn turns the phone.

For a minute all Sam sees is nylon fabric. When the image clears up, she realizes she's looking at a small tent, presumably in Dawn and Chad's living room.

Poking their heads out of the tent are their two adorable children holding a hand-made sign that says, "Way to go Aunt Sammy!"

Dawn flips the phone back. "They thought it would be appropriate to congratulate you from a tent. It felt like the right thing to do."

This sweet gesture of friendship and nostalgia is too much.

"Stop. That is the cutest thing ever!" she says. Tears are now trickling down her face.

"It's not big enough to get stuck between the walls, so Chad even let me put it up myself for old times' sake." Dawn laughs. At the sound of his name, Chad's face enters the screen. "Hey Sam! Congratulations on the store. We can't wait to come visit!"

"Hi!" She never saw Chad in her return to 2001, but he was still very much a part of her time there. "It's so good to see you!"

"Hey, what about me?" Dawn says in faux indignation, moving away from Chad so that she can have the screen to herself.

"It's always good to see you, Dawn. It feels like we were just having those special brownies a few days ago."

Dawn laughs. "Yeah, time is so weird like that, isn't it?"

About the Author
Stephanie Carey

Stephanie developed an appetite for books at a very young age. At one point her elementary school librarian said she was running out of fiction books to recommend to Stephanie because she had already read so much of the library. When she was in college at Milligan University, Stephanie worked at the student union grill serving up hamburgers and chicken fingers. The journalism professor at the school was a regular grill customer. One day, Stephanie decided to tell him she loves to write. He scowled at her and told her she probably didn't know how to write, but if she took his Journalism 101 class, he could teach her. At that moment, a journalist was born.

Stephanie went on to write for The Rocky Mount Telegram, and then into radio where she hosted Morning Edition and covered news in Evansville, IN. She explored a variety of jobs in the media sector before where she was inspired to one day own her own media company. In 2018, Stephanie became the co-owner and publisher of The Pitch, an alternative newspaper in Kansas City. Her biggest flex is that she kept it alive during the height of COVID. She sold The Pitch in 2021. She now works in tech sales and lives on The Country Club Plaza with her prison rescue dog, Frannie.

BLINDSIDED
The Soundtrack

Every great story needs a killer soundtrack.

Relive the emotions of 2001 with this carefully curated playlist containing all the bops that made 2001 iconic - complete with heartbreak anthems and nostalgic bops that will make you want to grab your butterfly clips and sing into a hairbrush.

Warning: May cause flashbacks to frosted tips and AOL chatrooms. Proceed with headphones. Highly likely to include the song that feels like heartbreak in the rain, the one you secretly know all the lyrics to, the one that made you want to text your crush on a brick sized cell phone.

Scan the QR code to press play and let the music transport you back, way back, back into time.

Acknowledgements

I want to thank my friends who supported me through writing this and didn't scoff when I said, "I'm publishing a time travel novel."

Thank you to those who took time to read an early draft: Stephanie Flores, Cherry Wolf, Brian Seymour, Anne Abernathy, Erika Welch, Amber Blouin, and Riley Saucedo. Your feedback was instrumental in bringing this story to life.

Thank you to Cynthia L. Robinson of LaunchCrate Publishing for guiding me through the entire process of publishing – from editing and pagination to my amazing cover design.

Finally, thank you to my mom, Teresa V. Mitchum. Not everyone gets a writing expert and "Comma Whisperer" as a mom. Thank you for your thoughtful suggestions and edits, and for being an inspiration to me as a writer my entire life. Was editing this book less painful than helping me with science fair projects in my childhood? I hope so.